LADY

OF

Jeffrey Manor

Book 4 of the Knights of the Castle Series

J. S. Cole and
Naleighna Kai

Macro Publishing Group
Chicago, Illinois

My Boss
To Dolores
From Author
J. S. Cole

Enjoy your Book

Lady of Jeffrey Manor by J. S. Cole and Naleighna Kai Copyright ©2020
ISBN: [Ebook] 978-1-952871-02-3
ISBN: [Trade Paperback] 978-1-952871-10-8

Macro Publishing Group
1507 E. 53rd Street, #858
Chicago, IL 60615

Cover Designed by: J.L Woodson: www.woodsoncreativestudio.com
Interior Designed by: Lissa Woodson: www.naleighnakai.com
Editors: J. L. Campbell jlcampbellwrites@gmail.com; Lissa Woodson, Brynn Weimer, Stephanie M. Freeman
Betas: Debra J. Mitchell, Ellen Kiley Goeckler, and Unique Hiram

LADY

OF

Jeffrey Manor

Book 4 of the Knights of the Castle Series

*J. S. Cole and
Naleighna Kai*

♦ DEDICATION ♦

J. S. Cole

I would like to dedicate this book to my children Jaiden, Jayla and Jaycee. May the story to follow inspire you to become better versions of yourselves. Love!

Naleighna Kai

I dedicated this book to:

Jean Woodson,
Eric Harold Spears,
LaKecia Janise Woodson,
Mildred E. Williams,
Anthony Johnson,
L. A. Banks,
Octavia Butler,
Tanishia Pearson Jones,
and Priscilla Jackson

♦ ACKNOWLEDGEMENTS ♦

I would like to give thanks to The Almighty! I want to give thanks to my husband, Mom and children who are the other half of my heart and the air that I breathe; the reasons why I do what I do.

Thanks to all my friends who cheered me on through this writing journey. Thank you to all the special editors, J.L Campbell, Karen D. Bradley, and the Beta Readers—Debra J. Mitchell, Brynn Weimer, Stephanie M. Freeman, Ellena Kiley Goeckler, Unique Hiram and April Bubb.

Also special thanks to my cousin, J. L. Woodson, for the beautiful book cover.

And last but not least, a very special thanks to my auntie the *USA TODAY* Bestselling Author, Naleigna Kai. When she told me that I was going to write a book, I thought she was joking. I've never written a book or actually aspired to. She helped and guided me every step of the way. I am forever grateful for her for giving me the opportunity of a lifetime. Thanks to the members of my Tribe who jumped in and did their thing to bring this to the finish line. Not only do I help save lives, now I can add the title of author to my achievements. Thank You!

J. S. Cole

Naleighna Kai

Special thanks goes out to: Sesvalah, J. L. Woodson (for the awesome cover designs for the Knights of the Castle and the Kings of the Castle series), Debra J. Mitchell, J. L. Campbell, Kelly Peterson, Janine Ingram, Ehryck F. Gilmore, LaVerne Thomspon, Kassanna Dwight, Vikkas Bhardwaj, Stephanie M. Freeman, Ellen Kiley Goeckler, Shae Cross, Unique Hiram, Siera London, the Kings of the Castle Ambassadors, Members of Naleighna Kai's Literary Cafe, the members of NK Tribe Called Success, the members of Namakir Tribe, and to you, my dear readers . . . thank you all for your support.

Much love, peace, and joy,
Naleighna Kai

One Love,

Naleighna Kai

Chapter 1

"My husband wanted an open marriage." Blair scanned the shocked faces of the family members standing in her dining room. "So, my best friend opened her legs and he landed between them. I opened the front door and walked out. He can be *open* all he wants. I won't be a part of it."

She moved a few inches past the entrance toward the identical triplets, her Aunts Dorothy, Dorsey, and Darlene. Those D's should have stood for drama since one was a varying shade worse than the other. Blair's meddlesome Aunt Darlene, the leader of the group, blinked rapidly at her confession.

"Now, does that answer your question about why my husband isn't at this farewell dinner?" Blair asked, then tilted her head slightly. "Or do you need more grisly details to gossip about when you go back to whatever corner of hell you came from? I've got plenty of them."

Ellena and Kamran, the guests of honor, had only been at Blair's house for twenty-nine minutes before they were forced to leave because of an unexpected and unwanted guest—Blair's grandmother, Ruth. Propped on a wooden cane with a cloud of platinum curls that glowed like a halo under the house lights, she was a vision of sweetness and light. Her face told another story. The muddy brown gaze seemed to crawl from one face to another, as a faint sneer tipped the corners of her lips. The cloying scent of musky perfume tinged with urine seeped into the air around her; announcing her presence while conjuring memories of broken bones and tears—mostly from the three daughters she had done the most wrong—Melissa, Ellena, and Amanda. The old woman was the one person that six relatives attending the farewell dinner never wanted to lay eyes on again in this lifetime or the next.

Aunt Darlene looked away and ran a hand through the short locs that framed her face which was the color of rich mahogany. "I'll mind my business from now on."

"Thank you." Blair shifted her gaze to Aunt Dorsey, who slid her designer glasses further up on her nose. "And why would you invite Grandma, knowing it was going to create nothing but drama?"

Dorsey's curls shifted on her shoulders as she tipped backwards, away from Blair's fury. "I didn't think Ellena could hold a grudge so long."

"It's not holding a grudge. All four of her children are dead," Blair shot back, trying to rein in her anger at the eldest triplet. "Grandma kidnapped them because their father didn't want to pay child support, was driving them to a man who she knew didn't love them nearly as much as his bank account, and then caused a car accident which resulted in their deaths. What part of that don't you understand? Then instead of giving Auntie time to process, Grandma just steamrolls back into her life demanding forgiveness. Not asking—demanding. I'd be upset too."

Blair's children sat on the sofa, absorbed in the adult drama. The rest of the family was silent for such a normally noisy clan. Most of her estranged father's family was present, but only a few members from her mother's side. Having them all there at the same time would be like putting a lit match to parchment.

Out of Ruth Hinton's brood of eleven children—one set of triplets, three sets of twins, and two single-born, only Aunts Amanda, Ellena, and Melissa seemed to be blessed with any common sense, compassion, or love. Blair's father Devon, Ruth's only son, had deserted her and her mother when Blair was just a baby, forbidding anyone in his family to maintain contact. When Blair was finally reunited with her father's relatives as a preteen, she soon realized that the majority of the group managed to make every situation all about them.

"That man didn't want his children," she reminded the rest of the family. "He wanted custody because it wouldn't hit his pockets so hard. And Auntie paid the price. So, get the hell out of here with that holding a grudge bull."

"Well, not speaking to her isn't going to bring them back," Dorothy said, leaving her sister's side so she was closer to Blair. "My Bible says that we are supposed to forgive one another. Honor thy mother and thy father…." she said, scanning the rest of the group for support.

"That's rich, coming from you. Same bible says something about not provoking your children to anger, guess you missed that part, huh," Blair shot back.

Amanda stepped forward and faced her older sister head on. "Time and distance gives Ellena peace of mind, Dorothy. The death of one child, let alone four, isn't an easy thing to bounce back from. You can't put a timetable on grief, forgiveness or betrayal. You of all people should understand that,"

Those two had always been at odds. Especially since Dorsey had been part of a plot with their mother that unfairly landed Amanda in a corrupt restitution center in the heart of Mississippi, when she should have been safe with her family back home in Chicago. Two men ended up on the wrong side of the grave, and another lost his eyesight, as an indirect result of their actions.

"I love you, both," Blair said to her aunts Darlene and Dorsey. "But if you ever invite that woman to my house again, when I explicitly asked you not to, you'll find yourself right outside the door along with her."

Dorsey scowled, not a good look on her. "Now wait a minute, young lady. I'm still your elder."

"Then act like it and respect my boundaries," Blair snapped, and didn't step back as her aunt intended.

Intimidation worked when she was younger, but now she was a grown woman and they had violated her home and the peace she worked so hard to achieve. As well as several family members she loved.

"If I say she can't be here, then dammit, that's what I mean." She inhaled and let out her breath slowly, as she noticed her cousin Christian gesturing for her to keep cool. "Messed up an entire dinner over this. It took so much to bring everyone together to say goodbye to Auntie Ellena."

Amanda placed a calming hand on Blair's shoulder. Blair covered that hand with one of her own. She loved this particular aunt, as well as Melissa and Ellena, so much.

Taking a page from Ellena's handbook, Amanda had also distanced herself from most of the family after an unfortunate incident involving Grandma Ruth. Blair had looked forward to having both Amanda and Ellena for dinner for an entire year, and Ellena's marriage to Sheikh Kamran Ali Khan finally provided that opportunity. Then Dorsey and Darlene had to pull this madness. Blair suspected Aunts Veda and Vivian had added their own fuel to the fire, judging by the way they were eyeing Amanda and Melissa with unbridled jealousy.

"Come on," Blair said, beckoning to her children, Bella, Lola, and Brandon, who scrambled off the sofa and were at the foyer closet before she could finish with, "We're leaving."

Melissa's son Christian, Blair's favorite cousin and partner in crime when they were growing up, whipped around to face her. "Leaving? But isn't this *your* house?"

"I'm going to let them have this one," she replied, gesturing toward the stairs behind him. "Could you go lock up my bedroom before something else comes up missing? Some folks believe those five finger discounts don't just happen at department stores." She gave Dorsey a pointed look. The woman could actually steal a radio and leave the music playing. "Mama, you coming?"

"Damn straight," Lela said, shifting a gaze to her sister-in-law, who didn't seem fazed at the havoc she'd wreaked on what was supposed to be a wonderful family gathering.

"Auntie Amanda? Auntie Melissa? Christian?"

"We're rolling with you," he said, stepping up next to his mother, who also nodded.

Dorothy tilted her head and peered at the group that was about to make a hasty exit. "Then who's going to serve dinner?"

"You're going to serve yourself," Christian answered, chuckling as he held open Blair's coat. "And clean up, too. You'll figure it out."

Blair slid her arms into the sleeves. "You managed to destroy what was supposed to be a happy reunion. All because you were selfish."

"I'm getting a little tired of your smart mouth, young lady," Darlene complained as Dorothy groaned an agreement. The triplets all had the same pinched face and hard eyes, but Dorothy was a little … wider than the other two.

Blair froze, then glared at her aunt for a few moments. "You know what? Better yet …" She left Christian's side, went to the closet, grabbed everyone else's coats, and spread them on the sofa and chairs. She felt like reenacting the infamous scene from *Waiting to Exhale* when Angela Bassett grabbed her cheating husband's clothes, tossed them into the sunroof of their luxury car and set everything on fire. The only thing missing was a match. On second thought, maybe a torch. Her aunts could weather some ugliness just as much as they could stir it up.

"Are you putting us out?" Darlene and Dorothy asked at the same time, their eyes widened in shock. Dorsey's hand went to her fleshy hip, as she waited on the answer.

Blair grinned as Christian helped slide off her coat, and hung it back in the foyer closet where it belonged. "See? And they're smart too," she taunted with a smile. "No, I'm asking *most* of you to leave. The ones who have drama as a middle name."

Aunt Dorothy whipped around, gesturing toward the spread of food that made up their intended meal. "What's going to happen to all this food?"

"Don't worry about it." Blair scanned the dining room table, loaded with what would be a week's worth of leftovers. The few people who would remain could not possibly polish off everything. "There'll be someone to help me take care of it."

Aunt Dorothy grimaced. "And I even brought my aluminum foil and extra 'to go' plates."

"Should go well with the air pudding and wind sauce just outside of the front door," Blair quipped as she waved her hand in the direction of the driveway.

Christian snickered, but Blair nudged him into silence. Aunt Dorothy was the one who gave anyone the side-eye if they went in for seconds. She had designs and well-thought-out plans for the leftovers and always came prepared, despite being warned against doing so. Today, she would have been disappointed anyway.

Blair gave Christian and Auntie Amanda a nod. They disappeared into the dining room to take their place at the table.

"That's cold," Veda said, sliding on her boots by the door. She and her twin Vivian still dressed alike, the same way they had growing up. "We can't even take some of it with us?"

"No, we shouldn't suffer because you don't know how to act," Christian yelled back, slipping into the room to stand a few inches from his cousin. "Blair and I planned this carefully. Even had me out there working the grill and it's cold enough to turn Corn Flakes to Frosted Flakes. Then y'all come along and dismantle all of our hard work in under five minutes." He held out his fist to Blair and she obliged by tapping it with her own. "Y'all don't have anything coming. Popeye's is still open. I heard that chicken sandwich is driving folks crazy."

Blair loved her cousin like no other. They had been inseparable from the moment Auntie Ellena came back into her life and brought Amanda and Melissa along, too. The rest of the family kept their distance for a while. They didn't want to anger Devon, the only male child, by getting too close with the daughter he had abandoned. But soon they were all a part of Blair's life, for better or worse. Blair considered aunts Melissa, Ellena and Amanda a blessing. The rest of them she called collateral damage.

Christian waved Blair's children to the table set for them in the kitchen. They rushed off, but Brandon, her oldest, paused at the doorway to look over his shoulder.

Blair nodded to let him know she was fine.

"That's so unfair," Darlene said, as Blair and the ones who were to remain for dinner moved around them.

Blair froze on her way to the table, then kept it moving. "Unfair? For once, I didn't want any family secrets or drama to grace the table with the rest of the food." She slid the plates from the stack and handed the first three to Christian who passed them on before taking from the next stack.

"What drama?" Dorsey shot back, folding her arms across a pair of breasts that hung so low they could help tie her shoes. "You're just being extra. Same way you didn't even want Grandpa or our husbands to be here for dinner."

"Extra? Oh, okay, let's go there." Aggravated, Blair dropped the last plate, nearly causing it to break.

Christian put out one hand to hold her steady.

"Let's talk about how Uncle Joe, grandpa, and others have run up on almost every female on your side of the family because no one, not a single one of you, made a peep about it. Ellena, Melissa, and Amanda finally had to handle that business because you all were more worried about saving face."

Blair crossed the space between them as two of the women tried to slow her down.

It didn't work.

"Now you've made it the children's responsibility for not going near those men, when those men shouldn't even be here in the first place. *That's* why they're not welcome in my home. And somehow you think I want to look out for Grandma, too? After she stood by and allowed it to happen?"

Christian's head whipped around to his mother. "Is that why we don't …?"

"No, he didn't touch me," Melissa answered in a low tone. "Not because he didn't try. I was pretty handy with a switchblade. So were Ellena and Amanda. That's where he got that cut on his thigh."

No one spoke for several moments after that admission.

"Then y'all want to get mad because I wouldn't let him or any of your husbands come here for dinner, pretending like we're just one big happy family. Then you also were mad at those who spoke out about it and those who managed to protect themselves."

"Every family has its struggles," Ruth Hinton growled, finally finding her voice. "We ain' no different."

"You're absolutely right," Blair shot back leveling a stony glare at her grandmother. "Uncle Joe called it keeping it in the family way. Uncle June called it 'breaking us in. Uncle Steve's "give me some sugar always seemed to turn into a bite that left marks, and a drive anywhere with one of Grandma Ruth's "special friends" meant having his hot sweaty hand on your thigh or elsewhere. All of them peeled dollars or fives off of some wad that smelled like cologne for a kiss or our silence. You pimped out the children in this family or condoned it by keeping your men. The excuses were always the same. They were just playing, or somehow we misunderstood their intentions. Either that or we were just flat out lying. Wasn't like you could get away from all the attention with all the of cousins piled in the front seat with him. And then there was your husband, well he liked to watch. Us in the bathroom, us playing hopscotch, he just couldn't keep his hands away from his crotch or ours."

"He was sick," Dorsey snarled, finally finding her voice. "He went to counseling at the church."

"Yes, of course," Blair taunted. "Uncle Joe and all of your husbands were sick. So sick that one of them spread their illness to Calla. You remember Calla don't you?"

"You leave her out of this," Ruth cried, shaking her cane at Blair.

"Why? You didn't. Kept her way from a lot of things. Except that one thing."

Blair scanned the faces of the women gathered near the front door who were stalling on making that exit stage left. The others had fanned out from the dining room and now stood near the living room entrance.

"Let me put y'all on notice," Blair warned. "The time for women and children sitting at the table with the men who hurt them is over."

She let that resonate for a minute, relishing the shocked expressions, and the feeling of solidarity as her mother, loving aunts, and cousin suddenly surrounded her creating a wall of protection.

"If you want to be around him, then you all can go to *his* house and eat. I don't want him, Grandma, your husbands who can't keep their hands to themselves, or any of the people who support them anywhere near my children." She grabbed their coats from Christian's hand and tossed them their way. "Now about that exit."

"You're going to regret this," Dorsey said between her teeth.

Blair gestured to the door that Christian now held open, only feeling bad for the fact that her children had to leave along with her. "Not as much as you will if you bring that drama to my doorstep again."

Chapter 2

"Why are you sending my son to America?" Yousef asked Sheikh Kamran Ali Khan, as he rubbed his salt-and-pepper goatee. His beard framed a round face with olive skin and that thick, silky dark hair—a Khan trait.

"He is the royal escort bringing certain members of my wife's family from the Midwest to Durabia," Kamran replied, inclining his head toward his nephew, Hassan. "And as an ambassador of Durabia, he will help acclimate Blair Swanson and her children to our culture on that lengthy plane ride."

Hassan noticed that his uncle didn't mention that Blair and Hassan had already become close through their daily virtual culture lessons.

Smart man, Uncle, very smart.

He took his new position as a cultural ambassador seriously. He hadn't expected to feel quite so warm about the feisty young woman with such wit, intelligence, and humor. He had never laughed so hard in his life, but she had also given him many things to ponder.

"You could have asked anyone to do that. It is a menial task," Yousef said, with a dismissive hand gesture as he leaned forward in his seat.

"True, but he has expressed interest in Durabia's expansion, as well as how to deal with problems related to the sudden surge of growth. We are now at twenty percent nationals and eighty percent expatriates. This means we will outgrow our capacity to maintain Durabia ourselves, and will always depend on outside labor and will have an influx of people from all over the world." Kamran shrugged and met Hassan's eyes. "What better way is there to introduce an American, especially one now directly related to the royal family, to our ways than by sending someone who has the knowledge of both Western and Durabian cultures?"

Yousef's chest heaved as though his frustration had settled there. He smoothed a hand over his tunic. "I do not like this."

"You do not have to," Kamran shot back. "Part of this transformation is having members of the Khan family actually hold a position that earns money, instead of simply being given so much as a birthright. Too many of them have Durabia's money at their disposal yet feel no responsibility to anyone but themselves. For too long, life has been one big party for them, with no consequences for irresponsible behavior." Sheikh Kamran shifted his stance, still unwilling to stay long enough to take a seat in the elegant parlor. "The time for that is done. A member of the royal family will welcome a member of my beloved's family."

"They are not royals," Yousef snarled, eyes flashing with anger. "She is a commoner. No matter how you dress her up."

"And that is your take on things," Kamran countered smoothly, his patience running thin. "And it is unfortunate, but it does not matter. Blair Swanson and her little ones will have all the rights and privileges that being married into the royal family provides." Kamran laid a hand on Hassan's shoulder. "Gather your things. You leave now."

Hassan nearly bounced with excitement, but managed a sober reply. "Yes, Uncle."

He had been looking forward to Blair's arrival. They had spoken sometimes multiple times a day over the past nine weeks, preparing for the transition from America to Durabia. He wanted to make sure everything was right for her, and came to enjoy their conversations about politics, religion, hopes, dreams, and even desires. The woman was amazing, strong, and beautiful. The pictures he'd seen of her in the dossier paled in comparison to the occasions when they used video conferencing. Her skin was the color of honey, and her soft brown expressive eyes slayed him.

She didn't like him at first.

From the one-word answers and the daily cross examinations, to answering a question with another dripping in sarcasm, Blair Swanson made it clear that his presence was merely tolerated. If he asked about her children, she grew distant. If he persisted, she cut him off.

"My children are my responsibility," she told him at the beginning of their nightly calls. "You needn't concern yourself with them."

At one point, their conversation had deteriorated to such an extent that she hung up on him. Undeterred, Hassan called back twice a day every day, sometimes just to describe the sunrise. Other times he called and left snatches of poetry, a random thought about a measure of music, or to tell of a fabric he'd seen at one of the open markets that he thought would look lovely on her. And then one day, miraculously, she picked up the phone. She never said a word, but the quiet on the other end was filled with her.

From then on, he spoke of summer dust storms and baked air that hung heavy with the sweet and savory spices. He recounted tales of thunderstorms so severe that they seemed to crack the sky during the winter. Hassan spoke of the water shimmering like a giant blue sapphire skimming the shores before racing down the horizon. Little by little their conversations slowly changed. Blair's questions about the schools and the local news gave way to the sights and sounds of his beloved country. Each night he described the sunsets from his side of the world, and she spoke of sunrises and rain showers that drummed on the roof of her car before she journeyed home to the children.

Evenings on Blair's side of the world involved bedtime stories for Lola, her youngest while Hassan listened on the other end as he enjoyed his morning coffee.

"Why are you being so nice to me?" she asked one evening as she settled in for the evening. "I wasn't very nice to you at first."

Hassan remembered letting the silence stretch between them afraid to hope and even more afraid to not answer.

"It's all right, Hassan you don't have to answer," she said.

He took in a deep breath then sighed.

"It does matter, Blair. You matter. I get the sense that you've been dealt a bad hand in life. Given the chance, I'd like to show you there's good in the world, too."

"But why me?" she whispered. "I didn't even have a kind word—or any word."

"Sunflowers," he said with a shrug.

"What?"

"Sunflowers search for the healing rays of the sun," he replied. "When it's dark, they turn to one another to share the warmth, to share the energy. Things are bleak where you are. Let me be that sunflower for you, Blair. Let me share my energy with you until you can step out into the sunlight once more."

Hassan put a hand over his heart as the memory and emotion spread through his entire being. The thought of being close to her, hearing her words carried on a whisper of breath as her sensuous mouth formed each syllable, made every nerve ending in him come to life.

"Wait, I would like to speak with Hassan alone," Yousef said, snatching Hassan's thoughts to the present.

Sensing that something was about to go wrong with this exchange, Hassan feigned an innocent expression as he said, "Oh no, father. Kamran is the Sheikh now. Anything you need to say to me can also be said in front of the ruler of Durabia."

Yousef pursed his thin lips in utter disapproval, glaring at Hassan. "Well, I do not…"

Kamran's eyebrow shot up, but his lips lifted slightly at the corners at Hassan's maneuver.

Yousef, realizing he would not be given the private audience he desired with the aim of talking his son out of this excursion, raised his chin. He made direct eye contact with his son.

"Do not involve yourself with this American girl in any way," he warned, gripping the edge of his chair. "You are promised to Imani of the House of Hakim and Sabah of the House of Yasin. You will keep the family obligation to girls who are pure and meant to bring you many babies. *Durabian* babies." He scowled, then spat. "Those American girls are loose—especially the …" He grimaced but left no doubt as to which Americans he meant. "No morals. No fathers, no brothers or uncles to see to their well-being. It is no wonder they come here seeking our riches. Do not soil yourself with their kind."

Hassan sensed his uncle seething with each word, but instead of showing his anger, Sheikh Kamran managed to say calmly, "Are you done?"

Yousef nodded; shoulders squared as though he was ready for battle.

Keeping an even pitch, Kamran said, "This girl—actually woman—

you speak of, is a beloved niece of your current Sheikha. A ruling queen who will now have a great deal to say about your commissions and accounts at the palace. A queen who bested one of the oldest rulers in the Middle East, and to this day he cannot locate his family jewels. A little humility might be in order."

All of the color drained from Yousef's face.

Hassan tried to keep his expression neutral. To see his father in such a state was a first, and well warranted. How dare he judge anyone in this manner? Especially since he had barely managed to escape Sheikh Kamran's judgement that came down on those who had taken part in a scheme that resulted in Sheikha Ellena and their four children being harmed.

"Blair Swanson is a surgical nurse with highly sought-after skills," Hassan said, stepping toward his father. "She will be working at the Durabia Medical Hospital, and she will receive housing from her aunt's private coffers and land endowments. She has no need of my money or yours."

"Does she know that?" Yousef growled.

"Careful uncle," Sheikh Kamran warned. "You are here and did not suffer everyone else's fate purely because I showed mercy. Please do not make me rethink my stance."

Yousef's lips parted; his eyes widened with shock before he clamped his mouth shut.

"I will attest to the fact that Blair is none of the things you claim." Kamran's gaze landed on Hassan. "You have a flight that leaves in an hour."

Chapter 3

"All you need is this little letter, right?" Antonio walked up behind Blair as she was getting out of the limo at a private airstrip not too far from O'Hare. A man of black and Hispanic lineage, Antonio had wavy cut hair, thick eyebrows, dreamy eyes, and a smooth face...all of which drew Blair to him when they first met.

"I don't have time for games, Antonio," Blair snapped. Her soon-to-be ex-husband had stalled the flight to Durabia for far longer than necessary.

She didn't know what he wanted. But for him to be hedging like this meant he definitely wanted something. The same way he was delaying their inevitable divorce, strictly because he was unwilling to let go. For the past few years, Blair had been doing all the work and he was reaping every benefit. Sad indeed that he wanted to have Blair *and* her best friend as part of the equation.

Blair had every intention of letting Netty have Antonio all to herself. She had tainted the marriage soil more than once—even managed to do so in their master bedroom.

"If I let you take them," he said with a sly smile. "Then I don't have to pay child support, right?"

"Whatever," she snapped, sighing as the children stopped playing long enough to glance in their direction. The caregiver her aunt hired was trying to keep them entertained, but they were growing restless after being held up for nearly an hour. "And the other shoe drops. That is what you're really worried about, huh?"

"So you'll sign something that says it, right?" He nodded toward the luxury plane. "If you're going to take my children out of the country, then I won't get to see them."

"Like you were seeing them in the first place," she countered, and he had the nerve to look hurt.

"That's not the point."

"That's *exactly* the point."

Antonio thrust the document toward her breasts, trying to brush his hand across them. "Sign this and you can be on your way."

She stepped back to avoid his pawing, but caught the papers before they landed on the tiles. "So, you finally hired a lawyer?"

"Yeah, you know." He popped his collar. "Protect my best interests and all that."

"Well that's what you do best." She scanned the dense lawyer speak on the page, realizing she couldn't make it to the plane fast enough to put distance between her and this idiot. "Protect your own precious hide even though it's not worth two cents."

He was the one who stepped out on her, with her best friend since grammar school of all people in the world. That one cut deep. But she realized now that she hadn't truly lost a friend. She'd never had one from the start.

While Blair was pulling double shifts at Meridian Hospital, Antonio was pulling double duty at two households. She was taking care of her three children, private schools, and household bills, while he floated all of his funds on sports bets, cars, and his "other" household, leaving Blair to fend for herself. Which she did—well. Now she was just tired. Even the job she used to love felt like more of a chore now. Nurses at Meridian were overworked and underpaid, almost to the point of instigating a strike. Not to mention, one of the supervisors was riding her ass because she wanted Blair to quit so one of her less than qualified friends could have the position.

With unwanted drama taking over every facet of her life, Blair was at a breaking point. A fresh start in Durabia was just what her life and her children needed.

"Sign it," he demanded, bringing her back to the unpleasant reality facing her.

Blair, who would simply let her lawyer deal with the unfairness of this move a little later, complied then asked, "Where's my copy?"

"You don't need one." He folded the page, preparing to tuck it in his pocket.

Hassan Khan stepped down from the plane and moved toward them. Blair froze at the mere power of his presence. He wore a long white tunic and pants. His olive complexion had a glow, and that dark, silky hair was shiny and cut to perfection. She had never favored a man with facial hair, but Hassan's goatee was trimmed in expert fashion. He walked toward her with the confidence of a man who had purpose and a plan. Her heart did a little leap at the sight of him, a man that she'd spoken with every day since Sheikh Kamran had honored her request for guidance.

Antonio was clearly just as affected by the magnetic presence of her aunt's nephew by marriage.

"Who the hell is that?" Antonio asked, jealousy etched in his tone and facial expression.

"That's for me to know, and for you to never find out."

Blair snatched the document from his hand, whipped out her cell and took a screen photo. "There. That should do it."

He frowned, clearly pissed, and said, "Whatever" then turned his attention back to Hassan.

No, he wasn't happy with that move, but she knew he wouldn't dare cause a scene at the airport. Knowing him, that piece of paper could come back to bite her. She might have been born on a day, but it wasn't this day.

"Come on, Brandon, Bella, and Lola. Let's get our seats."

Brandon, her oldest and most well behaved, gave her a wide smile, then took off and was at the stairs in a flash. Bella, her middle child, pulled her micro braids into a ponytail, then took her hand. Lola, the baby of the family, whose unruly curls refused to stay tamed, had her eyes glued to that big machine they were going to fly in. Her tiny hands clutched the pink butterfly case of her iPad to her chest. Neither of the children bothered to bid Antonio goodbye as they moved toward the plane.

Why would they?

After a short lifetime full of his broken promises and arbitrary punishments, for both real and imagined offences, their father hadn't earned himself a place in their hearts. Instead, the children poured themselves into schoolwork and friends, and took advantage of any spare moment Blair had to spend building blanket forts in the living room while they watched cartoons and pigged out on ice cream for dinner.

Blair threw him the peace sign, and moved forward.

Hassan's eagle-eyed gaze swept over Antonio before he kissed Blair lightly on both cheeks. He greeted the children before ushering them toward the guards that waited at the landing to escort them onto the jet.

"You did that on purpose didn't you," she said to Hassan, her skin still tingling where his lips had touched.

He placed his hand on her lower back to guide her to the base of the stairs, their position close and slightly intimate. "That's for me to know, and for you to find out."

Hassan winked and Blair threw back her head and laughed.

She could feel herself practically basking in the heat of Antonio's glare.

Chapter 4

Fourteen hours in a plane felt like an eternity. Blair watched as the children played or slept, while Hassan looked on and assisted where he could. In the quiet moments when the children slept, Hassan wordlessly took Blair's hand and brought her back to their seats which reminded her of a small den with all the amenities.

There, in those moments that the silence grew, their initial awkwardness gave way to a companionable muted calm that bathed them in the whispers of a newfound closeness.

"You're safe now Blair," he said in a voice above a whisper. "You all are. No more fear. No more pain. You're coming home and I am so very glad."

She smiled, searching his eyes for a moment. "May I ask you a question?"

"Sure, anything."

"Your speech pattern is so different from Sheikh Kamran's."

He peered at her a moment. "How do you mean?"

"He spoke very proper English, barely using any contractions."

Her gaze shifted to the passing clouds. "You actually sound like me sometimes."

"Ahhh, it's because I learned conversational English," he said, with a mischievous glint in those dark brown eyes. "My brothers, too. And I watch quite a few American television shows. I think the best way to understand a new culture is to learn about the arts and entertainment."

Blair laughed and the sound was magic to his ears. "Well, that explains it."

Hassan escorted Blair from his limousine into the foyer of what could only be considered a dream house. The six-bedroom, six and half bath white brick stone mansion was situated up a long pathway, on a grass-covered hill. The place was enclosed in a gated community and the Durabian skyline provided a beautiful backdrop.

He smiled as he opened the tall silver entry doors. Lola, her sunshine child, finally squirmed to be placed on the ground to go exploring. She hadn't let Hassan go while they were traveling on the plane, or when they'd arrived in Durabia.

Blair thought the outside was impressive but stepping into the foyer snatched her breath away. The spacious first level greeted her with plush furnishings. Cream walls with royal purple accents adorned the space. From where she stood, she could see a large parlor outfitted with children's games and toys. Hassan guided her through the living room into the dining room, then to the silver and white kitchen which led to a solarium and patio. From there, a kidney-shaped pool, hot tub, and deck were surrounded by trees for a bit of privacy. The décor was simple, but elegant.

When Sheikh Kamran asked what kind of lodging she preferred and her favorite colors, she had explained that a three-bedroom condo with some outdoor space for the children to play would be more than enough. This right here was beyond anything she could imagine. For some reason it had Hassan's touch written all over it. Very much a far cry from her humble beginnings in Jeffrey Manor—an area whose crime level had risen to a level that it had become a frightening a place to live. When she was younger, her grandmother once told her that Jeffrey Manor had been a wonderful place to reside. The steel mills were in full operation all the way from Torrence Avenue area and deep into the heart of the connecting cities in Indiana. Then the place boasted mostly of duplexes, with bungalows and stand-alone two-story homes around the edges.

Back then, her mother was the only Black in a school and area that was predominantly Jewish and White, all families of World War II veterans who had purchased their first homes and made their living from employment in the steel mills. The moment Blacks moved in, White Flight became a thing allowing Blacks and Latinos to live side by side. All was peaceful for a time, until the fabric of the neighborhood changed once again. Still her ex had insisted they remain there near his family instead of moving to an area that would be the springboard for a better life for their children.

This place, this … *mansion* was nothing short of overwhelming, but the very thing she wanted for her children to experience. The main reason she had done everything, even working two jobs and going back to school so she could bring in the type of income that would afford her—and her children—better opportunities.

Bella, Lola, and Brandon had already taken off in the direction of the parlor to examine the selection of games and toys.

Blair moved forward with Hassan right behind her, smiling as she took the spiral staircase leading to the upper level. The first room at the end of the hall was magnificent and had a masculine feel. The earthy scent that Hassan wore permeated the air and somehow complemented the warmth of their surroundings.

"I stayed here often while the construction crews built everything, and when the decorators came to put on the finishing touches," he said, explaining the presence of his clothing and personal items in the room. "Somehow it made me feel closer to you and the children."

She nodded, feeling warmed by the sentiments, then swept into three rooms that were obviously meant for the children. Each had their photograph on the wall surrounded by a gallery of other family members—both ones she loved, and ones she didn't at the moment. Clothing filled the closets, and the varied vibrant bedding fit each child's individual personality. Connecting doors went from room to room, but still afforded privacy.

"Someone put a lot of thought into making sure my babies would be reminded of home."

Hassan whispered, "Yes, someone did."

Blair left the last of the three connecting bedrooms and walked past a room Hassan said was a guest bedroom. They went to the far end of the hall into a massive bedroom that held a California King bed with luxurious silk bedding. The cathedral windows were shaded by a smoke-glass tint. She moved toward one of the doors near the bathroom and opened it to find a walk-in closet she could never fill. Silk tunics and pants in every imaginable color extended from the front to the rear of the closet, while the other side was empty as though waiting for her to fill it with what clothes she had brought with her from Chicago. Again, another level of consideration.

Blair was on the way to the window but paused when she spied a small gym to the right. For a few seconds, her jaw hung slack. Every piece of equipment she would possibly need was contained in the room.

"Who did all of this?" she finally managed. "Who could possibly know? It's as if someone looked into my mind and pulled out everything that I could imagine but hadn't put into words."

Hassan's dark brown eyes locked on hers. "At night I dreamed of you… turning our conversations over in my mind. During the day I'd live out those dreams by making provisions for you and your children. It was how I existed, counting the days until I might have you here."

He crossed the tiles to stand in front of Blair. His deep warm eyes penetrated hers. The air surrounding them suddenly surged with unspoken sensual tension. Their eyes remained squarely locked on one another, as if they were participating in a silent battle of the wills.

"There is an old saying among my people. Affection comes in at the eyes, enters the heart and flows through the hands."

Hassan took a deep breath, breaking the quiet exchange. "I selected everything here personally, the furniture, décor, gym equipment, even the clothing." His voice flowed over her like the smoothest whiskey. "There is security throughout the house and around the property. You are safe here."

Safe. She felt it all the way down to her bones. Something she failed to feel with the man she had married. The one person who was supposed to protect and love her.

Sometimes it was a smell or a sound. Other times, it was as simple as a song on the radio. The memories would pounce on her out of nowhere as the taste of saltwater and blood filled her mouth.

The nightmares all started from a simple outing to grab a cup of coffee.

* * *

She'd just gone out with a friend from high school and her friend's male cousin tagged along. When she made it back home a little later than normal, Antonio seemed upset.

After several slammed doors, drawers, and feet stomping around the house, she faced him head on. "What's wrong?"

"Who was that guy in the car?"

Shocked at his tone, and the implied accusation, she answered, "My friend's cousin, he—

"You're cheating on me with some random dude?" he snapped, glaring at her. "Pull your pants down."

Blair hesitated, unable to believe he'd made that request. She must have heard wrong. Antonio Perez was supposed to love and believe in her, not treat her as though she had done something that would destroy their marriage.

"I said, pull them down right now," he roared.

She hesitated and that seemed to anger him even more. His fists opened and closed as if he was having trouble holding on to his temper and was about to let it free on her.

Finally, she complied, quivering with a combination of anger and fear. Who was this stranger in their bedroom?

His eyes glinted with a fierce light. "Give me your panties."

Blair nearly choked, but managed to say, "Are you—"

Antonio tilted his head and his eyes flashed murderously. The fury and distrust on his face broke her spirit.

Tears streamed down her face. She was not that person. She had never been that person. Three years into the marriage she had realized he was the whore in the family. And because of his infidelities, he took out his insecurities on her—each and every time.

He put the panties to his nose, inhaled deeply, then grabbed her ponytail dragging her down a flight of stairs and out of the house.

She was naked from the waist down. Blair fought every inch of the way while screaming for help. None came. The only thing people did was watch. They streamed out from their houses and off the porch to witness as Antonio berated her over something she hadn't done.

While he railed at her and slapped her around, she didn't resist him.

The physical pain and agony in her soul was such that something deep inside her broke. She took the abuse, absorbing everything because she didn't want him to hurt her more than he already had.

Out of the corner of her eye, she saw Antonio's mother Olivia and his sister Jessica standing there in their pajamas looking on helplessly. When she reached for them, Antonio stomped on her hand.

"Why you reaching for them, huh? They're my family. They're on my side."

Olivia moved to speak, and Antonio turned on her.

"Stay out of my business, Mamma. Daddy had to discipline you a time or two for getting in people's business. Stay out of mine unless—"

Blair couldn't stand any more. She screamed, wanting the whole block to feel her pain and do something other than stand around watching. Maybe someone, some man, would intervene and tell Antonio this was not how a real man behaved. Someone who would remind him that he had a sister and a mother. Surely someone, anyone, would reason with him and ask him how he would feel if a man treated his female relatives the way he was treating her.

Submit to your husband. Your husband is the head of the house and you must obey. This mantra had been drilled into her head as a girl. Her father wasn't there in her formative years to show her how things were supposed to look. How could she possibly know that this wasn't some darker, lesser known chapter in the book of marriage.

After what seemed like an eternity, Olivia and Jessica had seen enough. They struggled with Antonio, freed Blair, and brought them both back into the house. He railed at her far into the night until he finally passed out, but even then she didn't sleep. She traced the path her life had taken to that point, and wondered what wrong she'd done to be humiliated in that way.

When she still refused to speak to him days later, Antonio apologized over his behavior. He promised nothing like that would ever happen again.

"I get so crazy when I think other guys are looking at you," he said. "I know I'm sick and I will get help. I want us to be a family. I don't deserve you, but I'm going to be a better man. I promise…I promise."

The bruises faded, along with the promises, but she stayed. Because of the children … because only the guilty ones and the cowards leave … because she wanted her children to have some semblance of a father, something she could never claim … because it was her house that she worked herself to the bone for… because she was ashamed … because she tried to leave and kept coming back … because this was her test, her sacrifice to be tried in the fire and come out as pure gold … because there was no testimony without a test … right?

The fear, the pain, and the hurt remained, even though she didn't outwardly show the signs. That day was the lowest point in her marriage. She was numb by the time she found out the second lowest point—him cheating with her best friend.

Netty didn't even bat an eye when Blair came to her.

Why, Netty? Why him, why my husband?

Netty shrugged as she slipped into Blair's robe and flicked her long red hair back from her shoulders.

Because I saw him first. You stole my life and had my babies. But now you can have the kids. I have him.

By then, she had already taken steps to gain her freedom. She'd asked herself, 'How do you take your hand out of the lion's mouth?'

After some thought, she answered the question herself. One inch at a time.

Safe.

The very sound of the word coming from Hassan, as if he knew this part of her past, soothed her soul.

Even better, Hassan's closeness and presence made her feel safe. More so than all of the security equipment in her new home. A stark realization settled on her as she stood there with him. Here was a man who would never humiliate her to feed his ego. Here was a man who would never put his hands on her in any way other than with love. Here was the type of man she could grow old with.

No, she whispered inwardly.

Hassan was there before her, and yet in a very real sense he was a world away.

He was off limits because their cultures were so different. He was slated to marry two other women. But in that moment, as her heart warred with her head, a stillness settled over her. He could have been anywhere in the world, but he chose to be there in the moment with her.

During the plane ride, he had taken great care to fully answer every question while offering suggestions to help Blair plan a strategy of her own. A strategy not only to transition into the nursing position that awaited, but also to become financially independent with the opportunities now open to her as a royal. Becoming a sponsor for businesses desiring to set up shop in Durabia would afford her more wealth than she could accumulate in years of working for a medical entity. She would forever be grateful to Hassan for opening her mind to those possibilities. Now she had both a plan and a purpose. Her children would never be poor. She would not leave herself at the mercy of a man who did not love, respect, and cherish her ever again.

"Thank you so much for this," she said, turning to face him after taking another panoramic view of the room.

Only a few inches separated them, and his eyes were intense as he said, "It is my great pleasure to serve you."

Blair gaze lowered to those delicious looking lips, wanting to know what they would feel like on hers. She closed a little of the distance between them. Hassan gently pulled Blair to him and placed a sensual, toe-curling kiss on her lips.

First shock, then pleasure swam through her body. The man's natural charm was in everything about him, and he hadn't shown any signs of being interested in her that way—though the opposite was certainly true.

Maybe she had been blind, trying so hard to rein in her unexpected feelings. She ignored the fact that Hassan may have had some of his own. The sudden tingle caused by his lips on hers made Blair feel like a high school girl with her first crush, then sprinted into the emotions of a grown woman exploring a realm of renewed passion. During the time they had spoken, she had come to admire his confidence and efficiency. He'd been caring and considerate, qualities that had been missing in her life far too long. As she stared into his eyes, one word filtered into her consciousness.

Love? Where did that come from? How did it happen so soon?

Blair didn't pull away. Neither did he.

"On the count of three," he said, locking a heated gaze on her. "Let's try that again, shall we?"

Blair nodded, too stunned to put a voice to what she felt. He'd already tilted her heart in the direction of love the moment he accepted her and her children into his life, without question. She hadn't known that a kiss could open the doors of her heart the rest of the way.

"One," he whispered, "Two, th—"

Blair's lips were on his before he could finish. The moan that escaped him was enough to send shivers of anticipation all the way down her spine, and tip the scale as it rode the wave back up again. His hands dipped to the curve of her back, keeping their bodies as close as possible as their lips and tongues explored. She could feel how much he wanted her; the body never lies. But it was more than just the physical, and that made this unorthodox connection powerful.

Love.

Yes, that was a real thing right about now. How the hell could she, a Black woman, and he, Durabian royalty, make something like this work? Especially given the fact that his family had definite plans for his life that didn't include Blair Denise Swanson.

With that, he pressed a kiss to her temple, then sauntered from the bedroom leaving her with a swirl of emotions and hopeful for her future. *What would Antonio think about you falling for this man so fast?*

With a satisfied smirk on her lips she answered herself: *Antonio who?*

Chapter 5

"Isn't it enough you people are taking our men?" Zaina, a petite, raven-haired supervisor snarled from the nurse's station. The group of nurses from different ethnic backgrounds went motionless, waiting for Blair's response. She had sensed the icy vibes the moment she walked into the reception area to start her first day at Durabia Medical Hospital. A far cry from the warmth this morning when Hassan's mother, Fatimah, showed up at Blair's home to make sure Bella and Brandon got off to school all right, and to keep Lola.

"*You people*?" Blair looked up from a patient's chart. "Please don't tell me you mean what I think you mean."

"Expatriates. Foreigners," Zaina spat, her round ivory face flushing with color. "Ever since your aunt married into the royal family, there's been more of your kind waltzing through the door acting like you own the place."

With one brow cocked, Blair asked, "And that's my problem, how?"

Another nurse, this time a red-haired buxom woman stepped forward. "Didn't Hassan Khan drop you off in his Silver Rolls Royce this morning?"

Whispers went up around them as the rest of the nurses stopped working and a few inched closer so they could lay ears on the heated exchange.

Blair gave Zaina a lengthy once-over before locking gazes with her. "And?"

"A soon-to-be Sheikh. Royalty," she explained in a tone that signaled she wanted to add an insult to Blair along with it. "You're receiving preferential treatment. That's how you got this position."

Now even more people crowded around, not even pretending to pay attention to their charts. The overhead speaker was announcing tasks that meant plenty of work needed to be done. Evidently, gossip and drama had taken the front row since the "new girl" had made it to their floor. Blair was going to make sure that every single one of them had a stadium full of seats and kept their nose out of her business. Hassan didn't let her roll around in Durabia unescorted. Whatever she needed, either he or someone he designated took care of it. But that was not their business.

She inhaled, placed the chart aside, then made sure her voice was loud enough for everyone to hear. "Incorrect. My getting the position has everything to do with my knowledge, hard work, and versatility. They don't hire second-rate folks here." Then she tilted her head and smiled. "Unless … well, isn't that how you landed your position? Because you were qualified, right? Or is it because *someone* has been sampling a little more than office coffee around this camp?"

A blonde doctor pushed a pair of owl-rimmed glasses up on her nose and gave a low whistle as suddenly several people found productive tasks to do.

"Damn, she has a point," a tall brunette said, leaning in to nudge one of the residents on her way to the elevator.

"I'm going to say this one time," Blair stated, scanning the faces of the people still focused on her. "My work got me through the door, my work ethic will be the reason I stay. If you think this hospital would put patients at risk only to please the Sheikh, then you don't have a good sense of what this place is about." Blair moved until she was mere inches from her target. "And another thing," she said, leaning in so that she and Zaina were eye to eye. "Wrap your lips around my personal business one more time, you hear?" She tilted her head, peering at the woman whose complexion had turned crimson. "Remember, sweetheart, I have options. You don't."

Blair turned, giving them her back to ponder as she prepared to start the day. Since this was bound to happen again at some point, she would have to remind herself that these women didn't pay her salary. While it was always nice to get along with co-workers, if they were determined not to like her for their own reasons, then they were going to be the ones with the problem.

You people? Seriously?

She put some distance between them as she made her way down the corridor and prepared for her first surgery in Durabia. The floors were concrete with linoleum on top, but as she walked, she noticed some type of cushion existed in between. Back home, the floors of her hospital were concrete commercial flooring. Definitely put wear and tear on staff members who worked on their feet all day. Blair had to change her shoes every few months and wear support stockings—which made her look more like a granny than a thirty-two-year-old woman.

Here, the cushion of the floors was a sign that someone had taken the staff's comfort into consideration. And the place had state-of-the-art equipment. Even the doctors worked from iPads outfitted with medical terminology to make it easier for them to communicate with the nurses, keep better records, and give critical instructions that wouldn't get lost in horrible handwriting.

Blair had a routine that settled her every time she set foot in an operating room. It worked well for her in Chicago and should work fine in Durabia. For some reason nervousness still set in at the start of every procedure, but she used that energy to make herself more aware, more attentive, more … conscious. The purpose of a surgical scrub nurse was more than simply passing scalpels, instruments, and tools. They also served as an additional pair of eyes against mistakes made through human error.

As Blair checked and rechecked the trays, the memory of Hassan came to her in the quietness. A smile chased the heat creeping up her cheeks. Maybe it was the way he gathered her to his chest when she exited his car, or the way he traced her lips with his tongue before finishing with a light peck. Whatever it was, she craved him.

If he keeps this up, my drawers are going to walk off my body and straight into his hands.

She chuckled at the thought and resumed her count.

The air in the operating room was set to a negative pressure point; an isolation technique used to keep bacteria and viruses from traveling to other areas causing cross-contamination in this sterile environment. The bright lights would be blinding if they were anywhere else. Here, they served to put special attention on every small detail. Sometimes a single element—missed or added—could be critical.

This place, with all of its advanced equipment—some she'd only seen in medical journals she read from time to time to keep up with advancements in her field—was a far cry from her origins in the emergency room on the South Side of Chicago. There, the gunshot wounds, motor vehicle accidents, traumatic injuries, and illnesses that escalated as a result of patients waiting too long to seek treatment, had consumed the majority of her eight years in the medical field.

But here, as in any operating room, each piece of equipment, each tool, each person, all factored in with judgement and efficiency, decided the success of any operation. Genetics, timing, and the fact that it was their time to remain on earth, did the rest.

Blair whispered the same mantra before every procedure. A mantra that had carried her through each process. A mantra that helped sweep aside all thoughts of family drama, concerns for her children, or the next personal crisis to manage. Even now, it swept out the thoughts and images of Hassan Khan who had consumed more of her head space than she thought possible. A mantra that had been the driving force behind her stark honesty in investigations and inquiries when a doctor was accused of malpractice.

She knew that staying silent could cost patients their lives. She was not having that in her operating room. Sometimes other nurses were too afraid to contradict doctors, but Blair had no such fears. She had a conscience that would haunt her if she didn't do the right thing. No job was such a concern that she'd forget one valuable thing … the very reason she stood in this room.

Blair's focus shifted to the task at hand as the rest of the staff took up their positions. A tall surgeon with an olive complexion and dark hair stood over the patient and said, "Shall we begin?"

She closed her eyes, and whispered the mantra, "The patient is the most important person in the room."

Chapter 6

Khalil Germaine slid into a seat facing the door and picked up a deck of cards. He shuffled them like a Las Vegas expert, dealt to the three empty spaces and himself while leaving a six-card kitty in the center of the table. His movements changed the entire vibe in Sheikh Kamran and Sheikha Ellena's Free Zone residence, which was nestled at the top of one of the tallest skyscrapers in the world.

The penthouse was surrounded by enclosed wraparound glass terraces, giving a spectacular three-hundred-and-sixty degree view to enjoy the sea and other sights of Durabia from the clouds. The accommodation was luxuriously designed, bold but well thought out, with spacious entertainment rooms, which included a fully lit onyx bar with lounge, a double height party space that featured a full-sized almond blossom tree. On the opposite side, the dinner hall seated eighteen with an industry-standard rear kitchen, so caterers had everything required to service a large event. The quiet areas included a glamorous library space, a study, a gym, and terrace pool. Some of their guests were relaxing in the more casual lounge with a cinema area as well as a convenient hidden kitchen.

Hassan had picked up Blair and the children to bring them to Aunt Ellena's for what was now the weekly gathering that brought all sides of the family together, along with the Kings and Knights of the Castle. These men were love-related, not blood-related, but were now an essential part of royal life in Durabia. After an assassination attempt threatened his life, Khalil brought together a group of his former students to discover who was behind the plot and to help him restore his organization to its primary intent. Khalil created the original Kings of the Castle organization for humanitarian purposes, but when he left on a spiritual tour his second in command brought in the worst elements—dirty politicians, the Russian mafia, American crime lords, and businessmen with their own sordid agendas. These corrupt members met their match as Khalil's former students—now aptly called Kings—dealt with each of his enemies accordingly.

Ellena's home overflowed with handsome men in either dishdasha—white tunics or business suits, women dressed in modest clothing, and children who were in another area being entertained by a group of teens from Hassan's family who were teaching them some Arabic words and games. Blair checked in on them from time to time, but she was at ease because her children were laughing and playing with all the others.

In the weeks and months since their arrival, she could see the marked change in her children. The smiles came easier and their laughter filled the hallways of their home. Even the tutors who came in marveled over Brandon's affinity for numbers and raved about Bella's ability to read on a twelfth-grade level. Reading had been their thing—every evening. She didn't even discourage her daughter from sneaking into the romances Blair favored from time to time. When she found out what Bella had been up to, she hid the "raunchier" ones and secretly replaced them with "sweet" romances instead. Once, Blair had done the same thing with sneaking into her mother's library. Blair smiled softly as she made her way back to the main hall.

Silence descended on the room and the Knights stood between the Kings, staring, slack-jawed and with wide eyes focused on the playing table.

"Khalil plays Bid Whist?" Daron, the technological genius of the Kings, asked.

Hiram, Knight of Grand Crossing, answered, "What does that even sound like?"

"Sounds like you're about to get your ass whipped, that's what," Shaz tossed out, as he nudged Vikkas in his side. The men, including Vikkas' brother, Jai, chuckled. The two were Khalil's biological sons, one of which he had reunited with thirty-three years after the Maharaj family had stripped Khalil of everything during a struggle for power and wealth.

Khalil glanced toward them, gave a little smirk, and nodded. Simultaneously, the Kings returned the greeting. The Knights, nine in all, simply shook their heads.

"I taught you all to play chess at Macro International, Pit, and the original form of Monopoly—The Landlord's Game." He sighed, tapping the edge of the cards in front of them. "One cannot stay in touch with anyone's culture if they don't learn about the people. Music, arts, dance, things that bring them together. You can tell a lot about a person by the way they play this game. All of this is important." Then his smile widened. "And yes, like Shaz said, someone is about to receive a good old-fashioned ass whipping."

Auntie Ellena walked in, her personal assistant, Saba, and bodyguards Rakim and Waqas in tow. Her husband, Sheikh Kamran, was by her side, a slightly older version of Hassan—handsome all the same. Auntie looked radiant dressed in a purple silk tunic and commanded everyone's attention.

Khalil's wife, Aashna, claimed the seat across from her husband and picked up her cards, waiting. Her complexion held a tint of rose, because she was certainly in on whatever her husband planned to do. Then she beckoned Hiram and Falcon, another Knight, to take a place as the opposers.

"Oh, that's cold," Daron said. "They're going to take on the young ones first."

Shaz came closer. Grant, Dro, and Dwayne gathered around as Khalil extracted Daron's signature fedora from his hands and placed it on top of his own head. The man looked positively too cool in that get-up. All that was missing was a cigar and sunglasses to round out the "card shark" appearance. Not to be confused with "card sharp" of the British variety which meant cheating. That was not Khalil's nature. He winked at Daron and said, "Now I have my thinking cap on."

Christian and Eric, Blair's brother, said in unison, "We've got next."

"Like I said, he's taking down the young ones," Shaz said with a chuckle as he looked at the two men. "You don't see any of us lined up to take that hit."

Khalil's focus left his wife and went to Christian and Eric, both of whom were just over six feet tall, muscular, bald, with golden skin a few shades lighter than Blair's. The cousins could have been mistaken for twins, except Eric always wore a serious expression and Christian's face seemed ready to break into a smile at any moment.

Hiram, then Aashna, followed by Daron put in their bids—the number of books they believed they could collect toward winning the game.

Khalil took the bid with a six low, meaning that all Hiram and Daron had to do to stop them from winning the game was make two books. He reached in to turn over the six-card kitty in the center of the table. Ace of diamonds, two of diamonds, King of spades, six of hearts, and a three and five of clubs. Mostly low cards. Cards that meant Khalil was already holding the best ones in spades and clubs.

"That's not a kitty," Daron protested. "That's a damn cat."

Khalil grinned up at him and said, "Me—Oooow."

Blair and Christian gave each other a look before they burst out laughing and everyone else joined in. They each had spent a little time with Khalil and realized that for a man who was so well-versed in all walks of spiritual life as well as the cultures of many people, he had a down-to-earth vibe that made him sought after for a great number of things—wisdom and advice being at the top of that list.

"Bid whist," Blair explained to Hassan. "It's like the chess of cards in Black families. Everyone doesn't start here, though." She glanced at her aunt. "Some of us are still hanging out at the kids' table playing spades, so ..."

"See, you're about to be put over my knee," Auntie Ellena warned.

"I'm too old for that," Blair shot back.

Sheikh Kamran's head snapped to his wife. "Am I to understand there is corporal punishment in raising children?"

Silence. And nearly every American in the room pulled a stone face.

"Ooooooh," Blair taunted, nodding. "We're not gonna talk about that, huh? Like that one time ..."

"Shush," Auntie Ellena whispered, grimacing but giving a warning glare.

"Don't shush me now," Blair shot back, encouraged by Christian and Eric's chuckles. "When we had to stand in the center of the room with our arms out for ... what was it Christian?"

"Two hours."

"It wasn't two hours," Ellena defended, glancing down at her pink fingernails.

Eric folded his arms over his massive chest. "You're right, it wasn't. It was a whole two hours and twelve minutes."

Khalil pretended to be into the game, but even he grimaced at that declaration.

"I do not understand," Sheikh Kamran said, settling into the space next to Ellena and putting a hard focus on first her, then Lela.

"We had to stand like this," Christian answered, holding his arms out in front of him. "And if our hands lowered, she was going to tear our butts up."

"No, that's not right," Blair declared. "However, many times we moved our arms, that's how many times we were going to be hit with that leather belt."

"You and Eric had it easier than I did," Christian mumbled.

"But … but that's torture," Sheikh Kamran said, eyes wide as his attention shifted to his wife, who was suddenly interested in the patterns of the carpet.

"Are you asking me or telling me?" Christian teased, as the Kings looked distinctly uncomfortable. Hiram, by the shaking of his shoulders, was trying—unsuccessfully—not to laugh.

"Ellena? Truly?" Kamran said in such a dismal tone that she couldn't look him in the eye.

"It was a difficult time back then," she said, then squared her shoulders. "And I don't spank children any longer."

Christian and Eric did a double-take. So did Blair.

"Don't be giving me the side-eye," Ellena warned Christian.

"Well, here's *my* side-eye," Blair shot back, folding her arms across her bosom.

"But it worked, right?" Ellena leveled a hard glare on Blair. "How many times did you get in trouble when you were with me?"

Blair almost laughed because her aunt did have a point. She was so grateful to have all three aunties in her life—Ellena, Amanda, Melissa. Something that almost didn't happen since Devon wanted none of the members of his family to interact with Blair or Lela. Only those three of Blair's aunts had defied that directive because fate intervened and allowed them to find Blair without Devon's help.

* * *

One day, while Blair and her mother were at a bus stop on their way to volleyball, a woman with reddish-brown hair was driving toward the stoplight, and yelled, "Lela."

Blair's mom yelled back, "Ellena?"

The woman pulled over. Soon they were deep in conversation, and Lela finally remembered to explain to Blair that this was her aunt, estranged due to distance and a rift within the family. She was excited to finally meet someone from her father's side of the family, and the love she felt for the fleshy woman with a honey complexion and wicked sense of humor was automatic, no question. Ellena shared how she had reached out to Blair's father many times to be put in contact with Blair, with no success.

Once Ellena found her niece, she became a big presence in her life. Ellena was the first call Lela made when Blair received that first tell-tale sign of womanhood. Ellena came to the house, picked Blair up and took her shopping for all of the personal items she would need for this new stage in her life. And Ellena's love was not limited to her bloodline. Blair's brother, Eric, was invited along for every single visit and experience. Little things like that never left Blair's mind.

As a teenager, Blair predictably began to push the boundaries set by

Aunt Ellena and her mother. After work, Blair would have a drink or a smoke with coworkers, staying out until midnight or later.

Once, when her mother was working nights, Blair figured she could come home in her own sweet time and her mother would be none the wiser. She walked into the house about two in the morning and Aunt Ellena was the one sitting on the sofa, waiting. Everything was a blur because that liquor had kicked in, but a belt coming toward anyone at top speed would be hard to miss. Blair couldn't move fast enough because that liquor was firmly running things. But the liquor did little to dull the sting of the belt on her behind, or the embarrassment of disappointing her favorite Aunt.

When Lela came home from work and heard Aunt Ellena's tale, they both threatened to send Blair to boarding school to put some distance between her and the crowd Blair regularly hung out with. That threat, and those taps on the ass, was all it took. Blair didn't give her any more problems the rest of those teenage years.

Unfortunately, adulthood was when the real fun began. That time, Blair almost ended up in the grave. Nothing like a near-brush with death to make a person straighten up and fly half-way right.

Blair blinked away those memories and frowned as she tried to remember the question.

"How many times did you get in trouble when you were with me?" Auntie Ellena repeated.

"Only once, Auntie," she whispered. "Only once."

"Exactly," she countered with a knowing smile. "So, get off my case. And because you all knew how to behave, that's how I was able to let you, Eric, and Christian roll to Great America by yourselves without any adult supervision. You looked out for each other and knew never to separate."

"Just so you know, there will be *none* of that kind of thing here," Kamran stated bluntly with a pointed glare at his wife.

Ellena tensed at his tone and seemed to shrink a little under the weight of these words and the intenseness of his eyes.

"Our children have already been through a horrific kidnapping ordeal," he added, referencing the fact that his family lost their minds when Kamran married Ellena and regained his status as next in line for the throne. His brothers made a deal with the Nadaum Crown Prince to take Kamran out of consideration. They failed on such a level that they, along with all the other men and women in the family who sanctioned it, were still paying the consequences. And it seemed they weren't the only ones.

Hassan, wanting to break the tension in the room, came to stand next to Blair. "So, who's going to teach me this Bid Whist thing?"

Khalil peered at him, then thumbed toward the second table in the room. "Spades first, youngster."

"But I thought you said that was the kid's table," Hassan protested, incredulous at being relegated to a lower status. "I am not a child."

"You have to crawl before you walk," Shaz said, clasping a hand on his shoulder.

"He knows Spades," Blair explained. "I taught him myself when we were on the plane here."

"For the record," Ellena said, recovering enough to take the empty chair next to Khalil, but putting a level gaze on Sheikh Kamran. "I'm all for giving an *adult* a spanking."

Hassan nearly choked on his lemonade as Kamran's olive complexion tinged with color.

"Too much information, Auntie," Blair said, shaking her head, chuckling along with Christian. "Entirely too much."

Chapter 7

The last weeks of October meant an end to the unbearable heat of Durabian summers. The occasional dust storms that came with the season filled the air with the scent of baking sand and spices. The winter season welcomed outdoor activities with an occasional interruption by strong thunderstorms that amplified the rich scent of the jasmine that filled terra cotta pots all over the estate. Hibiscus trees danced lazily in the evening breeze, seasoning the air with the promise of sultry evenings and pleasantly cool temperatures.

Khalil left the card table, stretched, then kissed his wife who giggled like a schoolgirl as he said, "Well, I think that's enough whoop ass for today. Let us allow someone else to win for a change."

"And he talks trash, too," Hiram said, grinning as he tossed the last hand of cards on the table. Defeated like everyone else. "What can't this fearless, larger than life man do?"

"But I can back up that talk," Khalil retorted, handing Daron back his hat. "Kamran, I'd like a word with you."

Hassan watched them, wondering what was so important that it had to be discussed during family time. The two men moved to one of the enclosed balconies, where they could have some privacy.

"I am going to America for a short while."

"How short, uncle?" Kamran asked. He didn't fail to notice the distancing move that Khalil made before answering. The breeze brushed across his face, a welcome respite from the day's heat as he patiently waited for his uncle's response.

"About a year."

Eyes narrowed, Kamran said, "That is not short."

He glanced over Khalil's shoulder at Ellena who smiled at some snatch of conversation. But then her gaze would drift away from the activity to the far window. That heart-breaking look remained. She still had moments when his family's betrayal haunted her.

"I am not ready. My heart is filled with so much anger at what my family did to her and my children."

Khalil placed a hand over his on the balcony ledge. "It will subside."

"Not fast enough. The ugliness of my family's cruelty is not easily forgotten," Kamran whispered, heart aching at what had transpired.

The truth had come out about why both of the Nadaum princesses that he married were mysteriously "barren" when it came to their marriage with Kamran as well as the involvement of his brothers in efforts to keep Kamran from becoming the Crown Prince of Durabia. His brothers and their wives then conspired with Sajid, the Nadaum Crown Prince, to kidnap Ellena and their four children because Sajid's sisters were severely punished for their deception. The end result was an experience so vicious that Ellena still would not speak about everything that happened to her. The one thing he was very aware of is that thanks to his wife, Sheikh Zoraib of Nadaum was missing a vital body part that hadn't been recovered. It probably never would be.

He sighed. "The treachery of my family runs deep."

"And you have taken time with your wife and children and given them the tools they need to heal," Khalil said, shaking his head at the servant who held up two glasses on the opposite side of the glass. "It is time for you to take your place on the throne. And there has never been a better person for the position. My role was only temporary, and to clean the house of all of your enemies. Unfortunate that they were all family."

Kamran shook his head, still concerned about having the balance he needed to truly be effective in such a high position.

"Because you started from the bottom and now, you're here," Khalil crooned, grinning and rocking to some unknown melody. "Started from the bottom and now your whole team's here."

Kamran chuckled and felt a bit lighter. "Aaaaand he knows Drake. The Kings told me a little bit about you."

"I say it all the time," Khalil said. "There is no better way to understand a particular culture than through its music, art, literature, and dance. That is where expression is uninhibited. So, I listen to all of it. Bob Marley, the son of a British Caucasian man and a country village woman, used his music to talk about the oppression of his people and made a huge impact all over the world. You, too, are now able to do so much more."

Khalil gestured to the area where Eric and Christian were now seated, playing against Daron and his feisty gun-toting partner, Cameron. "You are in a unique position to move Durabia forward spiritually. There is more money on this side of the world than in America, Britain, and all the places that are considered superpowers." He went back to the balcony and placed his hands on the railing, looking out on the towering landscape of the Durabian skyline. Cranes extended from the top of several buildings, a common occurrence since the economy was bursting and so was construction in all areas.

"The Bible asks, what does it profit a man if he gains the whole world and loses his soul?" Khalil said, keeping his focus on the skyline. "So many countries have no financial worries, but they are mired in darkness that costs them more than they realized. They are losing their souls, their connection to the Creator. Same with America, they are stagnant spiritually. Keeping women in an inferior status out of fear. Keeping people of color in low positions, instead of using that substantial wealth to eradicate poverty and help humanity. We have the money, the people, and the means." Khalil gestured toward the area where the main palace was situated. "Now you have unlimited power here. Do something. Be the example, Sheikh Kamran Ali Khan."

Kamran glanced behind them into the living room, where everyone shared smiles and laughter, and some good-natured ribbing. As he watched, Hassan reached for Blair's hand and she flowed into him, resting her head on his shoulder.

"There is growing concern within the Muslim community. My marriage to Ellena has set a trend," Kamran admitted, keeping his gaze on Hassan and Blair. "If marriages to expatriates continue at this rate, there won't be enough Durabian marriages to keep our population stable. They feel that I have set the wrong example by marrying a Black woman, an American, a nonbeliever."

"I think it sets exactly the right example." Khalil's gaze went to the couple. "For tolerance. For religious freedom. For love. Look at how you came together. What are the odds? You, of all people, know and believe that was Divine timing."

He looked out again at the Durabian skyline. Kamran loved his uncle, one he didn't know existed before a few months ago. Khalil Germaine Maharaj had been forced to give up his wife and child when he chose spiritual pursuits versus engaging with the Maharaj family credo of money over everything else. He had lost so much at the early stages of his life when he was forced to accept the family's judgment and the new life they paved for him. Only after bringing together the nine Kings—men of all ethnic backgrounds and religions—did he regain everything that had been taken.

"The concern among old guard Muslims is that the Durabian bloodline will cease to exist. How do I combat that?"

Khalil went silent for a few moments, considering his statement. "Compromise. For now, to accommodate those who are of marrying age, Muslim men can—at most—marry one expat for every two Durabian women and still receive the national benefits. That way, people marry for both love and for cultural stability. Then the Muslim world will not be as worried about what is going on here."

They both watched as Hassan guided Blair to one of the sofas and curled her into his arms. She closed her eyes and buried her head in the wall of his chest. The love and happiness coming from them was a beautiful thing.

"Do not approach this situation like our fathers and forefathers," Khalil warned, his gaze also on the two lovebirds. "Do not become like the American White male—so fearful of losing, that it takes over every aspect of his life. Find the balance between progress and poverty. Mentor your nephews to become balanced. Show them the beauty of not making their lives about thirst for power that destroys the soul. Show them how serving mankind and each other will bring greater joys. The Kings and Knights are the best example of that. They helped me in America. Put them to the task and let them help you here."

Kamran said, "You leave tomorrow."

Khalil grasped Kamran's hands in his own. "You are ready. You have *always* been ready. Step into your power. Your first test as Sheikh is going to be navigating the effects of this relationship between Blair and Hassan. His father, very much of the old guard, is going to fight them every step of the way. You cannot play favorites on this so soon after your marriage to Ellena. They will have to navigate the nuances of their permanent arrangement themselves."

Chapter 8

Blair reached into her scrubs the moment her phone vibrated and beamed at the image of Hassan on the screen. "Hello, you."

"Greetings, jamila," Hassan said in a low, sexy growl that sent a shiver of warmth through her body.

She tilted her head down so no one would see the huge smile on her face at his use of the Arabic word for beautiful. "Why thank you, handsome."

Every bit of the man's six-feet-three-inches of chiseled handsomeness started to grow on her and get under her skin. Love had slid in the back door while she was watching for it to come through the front.

"How is your day going? I was hoping you would pick up the line so I could let you know I'm bringing lunch. Are you hungry?"

Blair made her way toward the break room, her stomach growling at the prospect of what he had in store. "Yes, I'm starving actually."

"What were you thinking of ordering for lunch?"

You. You'd make a full meal. Instead, she said, "I wanted to try that seafood restaurant down the street from the hospital. But I'd skip on you bringing lunch if you'd fix me something for dinner."

"I would love to cook for you, beautiful. Didn't someone say that the way to a woman's heart is through her stomach," he teased, laughing.

"So, we're being *super* forward now." She adjusted her direction, aiming for the locker room to grab her wallet. The man was an excellent cook. Fatimah had taught him well. But Hassan had figured out that the way to her heart was actually through her children. They loved him. And for a man who didn't have any children of his own, he knew all the right ways to take care of them. Her, too. Having a man manage the details of her life was foreign, but Hassan made everything seamless. Another reason to fall in love with him.

"No seriously, I can grab you something for lunch, and still cook something tonight," Hassan insisted.

"No, one or the other, my friend. I'm not going to have you spoil me rotten." A message popped up on her phone. Hassan had sent money through an app.

"That should cover your sandwich."

"Thank you," she said, shaking her head. "You are too kind. You know, you didn't have to do that."

"I know, but I always want to make sure you are well taken care of." His voice was pure warmth and silk and hearing from him was sometimes the best part of being at work. "I hope you have a good rest of your day jamila."

"Stay out of trouble," she teased.

"Me? In trouble?" His voice took on an innocent tone. "Do you know who you're talking to?"

"That's why I said it," she shot back, laughing.

"Tonight, jamila."

He disconnected the call and she placed the phone to her bosom before taking in a deep breath, then made her way out of the locker room. She had a lunch date with either a tuna fish sandwich or chicken salad. But her taste buds and stomach were already at home seated at the dining room table, waiting on him.

* * *

Hassan also made sure that Blair was included in the social events of Durabia. This Friday night event was an engagement party on a luxury yacht. Blair caught her breath at the breathtaking view of downtown Durabia from the yacht's tall windows. The inside space glowed magically with blue lights rimming the dance floor. A beautiful fourth tier deck allowed people to enjoy the view, and a bar on every level with double sided buffets made sure a drink was never far from hand. The temperature had settled into a balmy eighty degrees, a milder variation of the sweltering heat that hit them earlier in the day.

He looked dashing in black blazer and slacks, and she, without knowing that he was suited in that color, wore a black dress that embraced her curves. They definitely complimented each other, and several people took notice. Some even went as far as asking if they were now a couple.

Hassan's answer, since her divorce wasn't official, was that they were friends. The pause he took before saying it left the meaning open for a slight bit of interpretation.

The buffet style dinner had everything: twice cooked beef short ribs, roast salmon, and tilapia, roasted vegetables, salads, and other delicious menu items. Sparkling lights shimmered above, giving the dance floor a disco vibe. Many guests were enjoying the good music from a live band belting out everything from Earth, Wind & Fire to current American and

World pop hits. The dance floor had always been her escape from real-world situations. Once she started moving and that beat traveled up her spine, stopping was not an option. Tonight was different.

With Hassan holding her in his arms, swaying with her to the rhythm of the music, she didn't want to escape anything. She felt safe. She felt … desired. At first, she had wondered if she was reading too much into this, but his actions continuously suggested otherwise. They were the life of the party at the beginning because so many people were curious about them. Then they became the subject of curious stares and soft whispers when they found a way to distance themselves to have a few private moments. One would have thought it was their engagement party.

The electric energy between them was undeniable. Even with words still unspoken, Hassan and Blair knew their feelings were real. This unexpected love felt like a gift to both of them, but there were many who were lurking to put a stop to their growing feelings.

As they stood by the rails watching the moonlight glinting on the waves, a short man with a thick mustache interrupted them. "Hassan, I haven't had the opportunity to talk to you before this moment." His dark eyes gleamed as he looked at Blair. "And this is …"

After the introductions were made, the man Hassan introduced as Idris asked, "Rumor has it this lady is yours. Is there any truth to what I've heard?"

A smile crossed Hassan's face. Then he said, "Tonight is for celebrating the happy couple … not for dispelling what might be unfounded rumors."

"But she is not one of the women you are supposed to marry," the man said, glaring at Hassan. "Why is she here?"

"I hope you enjoy the rest of the party."

The finality in Hassan's words made the man bow and back away, while Blair hid a smile. Not only was this man caring, he was quietly and firmly protecting her reputation.

After that night, Blair and Hassan were on everyone's social media page.

This didn't set too well with Hassan's father, who was adamant about his son marrying within their culture. There was no way, while he was still breathing, he'd accept a Black woman as his daughter-in-law. He'd take whatever measures needed to ensure that his cultural ideologies were followed by his son.

Chapter 9

The moment Fatimah made it home to make dinner, the drama started. And it wasn't the lightweight kind, either.

"You are aiding the situation of Blair becoming part of this family," Yousef accused his wife.

Fatimah closed her eyes then opened them to lock in on her barrel-chested husband. "What are you talking about?"

"I am talking about you; you are over there, every day, playing grandmother to her children."

"Why is that a problem," Fatimah shot back. "I have nothing else to do around here, so why should I not help out? Your attention is always on your other wives—your much younger wives. So why does it matter if I am not here."

"You are my wife," he roared. "You should be where a wife should be—in this home!"

"What does it matter, you have not been to my bedroom or touched me in any manner for years. I am a pariah around this place. And now I have a purpose that has nothing to do you—or those women who have made it painfully obvious that they despise me."

"I will …" he inhaled. "I will speak with them."

"Again," she snapped. "Do not bother. My son has asked for me assistance and I am more than happy to give it. There, I am appreciated. Her aunt is married into this family, or did you forget." Fatimah left him standing in the center of their living area looking lost, while she went to go prepare herself for the next day with Blair and the children. Such a joy. If her husband had his mind set, he could forbid her from seeing them at all. That would be unfortunate. Ever since Yousef took on two younger wives, the household had been pure chaos. She had lived with an unhappy marriage for her entire life. If her sons could have a better life, she would do everything in her power to make that a reality.

She felt the heat of Yousef's gaze on her but didn't dare look back.

* * *

Hassan dropped off his packages in the foyer and moved further into the house where Blair and the children were baking an American dessert with his mother. He greeted them in Arabic and everyone, even the children, returned it in kind.

The sunshine girl, as he called Lola, had her arms raised for him to pick her up as his mother glanced up at him and smiled.

"I did not know you were here."

Fatimah swayed slightly as she said, "I came to help Blair with the children. We're just finishing up."

"Are you all right?" Hassan asked as he advanced into the kitchen.

"I am fine." Fatimah placed the oven mitts on the counter. Something seemed off, but she gave him a warning glare that said not to pursue the question any further. He wouldn't, with her. But he planned to bring it up with Blair at the first opportunity. His mother had seemed happier ever since she had been coming here to Blair's home every day. Sometimes it felt as if she didn't want to go home.

Hassan closed his eyes and inhaled the scent of fresh apples, cinnamon, and another spice he couldn't quite name. The children were all demanding his attention, and he embraced each one before they ran back to their places at the counter. Well, all except Lola, who stayed within his arms.

"It smells really good in here," he said to his mother while tweaking the sunshine girl's nose and causing her to giggle. "What have you all been up to?"

"I baked an apple pie, it just came out of the oven," Fatimah said with a smile as Blair stepped into the room. "You two, go on outside on the patio. Is that not why you are really here? You do not need to sit around chatting with this old woman."

Hassan's olive complexion tinged with color. "Thanks, Mother. No old women here; only beautiful ones."

"You charmer."

Blair's eyes widened at the sight of Hassan. She pulled her silk robe tighter around her body as he came closer.

"Good afternoon, Blair, my jamila," Hassan whispered directly in her ear.

Blair inhaled and closed her eyes. "You always smell so wonderful. I didn't know you were coming over this early, I would have freshened up."

"No worries," he said, locking a heated gaze on her. "You look ravishing, as always."

"And such a way with words," she teased. "I swear you've been reading romance books all your life."

"Romance? Just because I said the word ravishing?" He grinned. "I think I need to read a few and brush up on more vocabulary."

"You'll have to find the books in Bella's room."

"Bella? Isn't that a little above her age?"

"She thinks she's sneaking into my stash," Blair answered, whispering it directly in his ear. "She doesn't know I'm putting those there deliberately."

She poured two glasses of lemonade and passed one to him before they made their way out to the patio. He glanced over his shoulder at the pie that was proudly displayed on the counter.

"Later, Mr. Sweet Tooth," Blair teased, nudging him to keep moving.

Hassan gave her a sheepish smile. "I was just checking the results."

"You were lusting after that apple pie." She took a sip of lemonade.

"Busted," he said with a shrug. "Lust, another one of those romance novel words?"

Blair burst into laughter.

The sunlight beamed brightly, illuminating the towering landscape of the Durabian skyline as they stopped at the edge of the patio.

"The scent took me back to the day we were on the phone before you moved here."

"Oh really." Blair smiled at him over the rim of her glass.

"Where we talked about your hopes and dreams and you revealed all the good things you wanted to accomplish. You said that more than anything, you wanted time to do things with your children, like bake and go to parks and things of that sort."

"You have a good memory," she whispered. "I also remember you telling me how you couldn't wait to meet me and how there was so much in store for me. I didn't realize that I would be walking into my dream home right away." She turned to him, tears of happiness streaming down her face.

He lifted her chin with his fingertips, brushing the tears away. Filled by the fact that so little meant so very much to her. Only one other thing besides his father stood between them. "Blair, you are a wonderful person, inside and out. You deserve the best for yourself and for your children." His warm breath caressed her skin. "Please handle this issue with your husband. Let it go. Let it all go and free yourself from this cycle of anger and abuse. The divorce is how he's controlling you. You don't need his child support. You don't need the court to force him to do right by them or you. Drop that demand in the divorce," he warned. "I will care for you and our children. I know how to take care of my new family. You are my family. The children are mine, too. This is hurting them."

"My lawyer is very adamant. He says he's supposed to do right by his children, and he should." Blair insisted, pulling out of Hassan's reach.

"He has not in all this time," Hassan countered in a calm tone. "You cannot force him to do the right thing. And holding on is making you bitter and angry." He took her hand gently and guided her to sit next to him. "When you're ready to let him go and trust that you will be fine, and *our* children will be fine, that is when you will be free. You have to trust me, jamila."

Blair inhaled sharply; her eyes filled with sadness. "It's the principle of the thing, Hassan. I know it doesn't make sense, but it is. We are grateful to have you and your family in our lives. I'm not even going to lie, but a steady diet of gaslighting, broken promises, and bones can make a girl gun-shy." Blair shuddered and ran her hands over her arms. "Poor choice of words. With a few drinks in him, Antonio thought Russian Roulette was high entertainment because he was the one holding the gun."

Hassan moved to reach for her. He froze when she shrank away holding a finger to her lips.

"When Auntie Ellena—"

"Sheikha Ellena," Hassan corrected.

"She'll always be Auntie to me."

Hassan smiled and some of the tension seemed to seep out of her expression. "Fair enough."

"When she told me that she gave you my number," Blair continued, "I was a little upset because I was not in the mood to speak to anyone—especially some strange man."

"Yes, I remember. So, was I that strange, eh?" Hassan frowned, feeling slightly insulted.

"You were then."

He shifted his chair to face her. "And I'm not now?"

"Definitely not now," she said, her voice husky with promise. "But after what I've been through, it's hard for me to …"

The catch in her voice caused a surge of protectiveness and affection to well within him.

"You are broken," he said to her. "I can feel the shards of you beneath your surface, cutting you … but also cutting me. You've been brave for so long … so very long. There aren't enough tears in me for what has happened to you." He paused, noticing that her eyes were filling once again. "You were right to retreat behind a wall; to hurt … to hate. You learned how to function for yourself and your children." He placed a hand over hers. "You were brave … *are* brave, but the memories are still there. The scars still ache. So here I am, extending a hand. For every second of fear and remorse and doubt. For the broken pieces that shift around inside you like shards of glass, still slicing at your resolve and your self-esteem. You want to believe that there is something more. I cannot give you back the years, or take you back to a time when life didn't hurt or disappoint. I didn't do the thing that still makes you cry. But if you ask it of me, Blair, if you want me to, I will apologize. I will take responsibility for all of it. All I ask is that you trust me."

She absorbed his words, her bottom lip trembling in an effort to contain her emotions as she buried her head into the wall of his chest and sobbed. "I'm scared Hassan... so scared and so tired."

Hassan clasped his arms around her. "I know, but maybe you can share the burden. Or at least let me walk alongside you."

After several moments had passed, she lifted a teary-eyed gaze to him and whispered, "All right."

Chapter 10

The next evening Hassan took a chance on giving Blair a call. He had been thinking about her all day, but wasn't sure where they stood after the intensity of last night's conversation. Usually he left a message and waited for her to call back. The night before, she mentioned that coworkers were still giving her a hard time. Now he was the one making things difficult.

"Hello handsome," Blair said, answering on the first ring.

"Hello jamila," he replied, and couldn't help the grin that lifted his lips and the relief that filled his mind.

"Hi," Blair greeted Hassan again, then added, "I said that already, right?"

They both laughed because they sounded like teenagers. Something about her made everything within him smile and the world felt all kinds of all right. He walked around the living room and settled on a comfortable chair out of earshot of the kitchen where his mother was preparing dinner and the children were telling her of life in America.

"I am sorry if I came on strong last night or spoke out of turn. I didn't mean to upset you … the last thing in the world I want to do is hurt or upset you."

"I know you didn't." A ping interrupted the silence before she continued, "I'm sorry, too. It's just that I still don't believe Antonio should get off scot-free of his responsibility."

"I understand, but remember what I told you about freeing yourself?"

"Yes, I do," she said in a grudging tone.

"How is work today?" he asked, changing the subject.

"Okay, I guess," she said, but the normal enthusiasm was missing from her voice.

He rose and moved around the room, perplexed by her willingness to stay tethered to someone who meant her, or the children, any good. "You are a strong person with a powerful personality. The best way to deal with a challenging situation is to change how you perceive it and how you react to it. You have dealt with even tougher experiences, jamila."

Blair exhaled and he hated that she sounded so weary. "I understand what you're saying, Hassan, but they're really trying me. And I don't want the patients to suffer from my failure to be a little less vocal and a lot more patient. A moment of second-guessing could cost a life, all because my co-workers aren't feeling the person giving the information to them."

"You do not have to work," Hassan said, well aware of what her financial portfolio looked like these days. He stayed on top of her accounts as thoroughly as his own, and made sure he was in a position to take care of her and the children and not the other way around.

"No, I don't, but I do enjoy this job," she countered. "The people though, not so much."

Hassan gave it some thought. "Sometimes you have an edge that automatically puts people on notice. Your guard is up. Even with me. Do not lose yourself in the process of trying to accommodate others. People take issue when they can't seem to get a handle on you." Hassan stroked a finger across the surface of his phone and her picture materialized on the screen. "Ignore them if you can, be firm when needed, and if you have to take it to management, then go there. But do try to be a little more tactful, jamila."

"Tact? What's that?"

He grimaced and tamped down on his reply.

* * *

Maybe Hassan was right. She had a hard time making friends after the one she'd had betrayed her like no other.

Blair could come off a little strong at first impression. She was blunt but was never disrespectful. She kept her guard up and sometimes pushed people away if they came too close. That being said, she kept a small circle of friends and tended to mind her own business. That kept everyone happy.

Netty, the most damning of all betrayals, changed all of that.

They were friends from high school until a year ago. They had celebrated birthdays together because hers was a day before Blair's. When Blair heard that Netty's husband was cheating on her with someone from Antonio's family, she did what any best friend would do and clued her friend in. The affair had been going on for nearly a year before Blair caught wind of it. Netty soon became distant, and at times a little hostile, as if her husband's betrayal was all Blair's fault.

Blair spoke to her mother about the issue because she was a little tired of being on the receiving end of Nettie's nasty attitude. Blair didn't have any intention of interfering with a marriage and a family that had been together all that time and didn't seem to have any outward issues. Though Blair had not witnessed the infidelity firsthand, she knew a friend would tip off a best friend to be on the lookout for strange happenings. She soon learned that most people loved living a lie.

The night the entire group of friends went for a girl's outing at a downtown club was the beginning of the end. Blair didn't do the "phony" or "fake" thing. A friend would communicate if there were issues, but that was beyond Netty's understanding. So, Blair gave her friend the same treatment she'd been shelling out. Soon, they weren't talking at all. Blair was usually the one who wanted to talk about the problems or issues in any situation, but when it came to a point that she didn't care anymore—it was a wrap.

The minute Netty showed both sides of her behind in front of the group, Blair didn't care anymore. She wasn't kissing anyone's ass. And the fact that letting her know about her husband caused her to disappear, meant Blair's heart pumped purple piss for her.

That kind of betrayal cut deep. So maybe Hassan had a point.

"Thank you, Hassan, I really need to hear this, especially from you. Even though you sound like my mother. Probably why she likes you."

"Oh, come on, jamila. What's not to like?"

They shared a snicker.

"Oh, I forgot to tell you, your sunshine girl is quite entertaining."

"Oh lord, what did she do now," Blair said. "That baby is one of a kind, I tell you."

"She sure is, but she did not do anything, it is what she said." He couldn't stop the edges of his mouth from curling upward.

"Do tell?"

"I was teaching her the American alphabet when my mother asked her if she could come and help prepare the dining room. Her response was. "Oh, I am so dizzy right now." Hassan peered into the living room where the children were entertaining Fatimah. "My mother could not do anything but laugh when she realized she meant busy, not dizzy."

Blair laughed. "Oh, my goodness, that sounds like her, she gets her vocabulary from my mom."

"She's adorable," he said. "I know you only have a short break, so you need a little Blair time to yourself before you get back to work."

"And he's considerate, too. What a catch," she teased.

Hassan deepened his voice. "Have a good night, jamila."

As he put away the phone, he thought about what his future might look like if Blair was a permanent part of it. How would they get around the things that stood in their way?

Chapter 11

Four months passed and the tensions with Hassan and the tribunal of Muslim leaders that were convened by Hassan's father, had escalated to the point that Khalil had been called in by Sheikh Kamran. He invited Hassan and Blair to his palatial home to talk about the not so subtle developments in their relationship. He'd been sent several photos from social media postings and comments about them from their more recent outings. He guided the couple into his living room, gesturing for them to have a seat on an off-white leather couch across from a television screen so wide there didn't seem to be an end in sight. After pouring Blair a glass of chilled Moscato d'asti, he settled on a cream accent chair adjacent.

"A lot of people are starting to get into your love life, yes? Yacht parties and social media are an understatement."

"Seems that way," Hassan said, as he took Blair's hand in his.

Khalil lowered his gaze as he took in that move and smiled.

"Can a marriage between two people with such different religions be successful?"

Hassan paused a few seconds before answering, "Depends on the strength of their faith and what they genuinely believe. If the people are not actively practicing, it won't matter."

"But that is not the case here," Khalil hedged. "Most times it means compromise when conflicts arise. It might also mean converting or ending the relationship altogether."

He let that marinate for a moment before meeting Blair's eyes. "I would like to hear your thoughts."

Blair gave Hassan a wary glance before answering, "Sure, I've seen it work in a twenty-year marriage and counting. My great grandparents were Muslim, may their beautiful souls rest in peace. But I also know die-hard Christians who divorced after less than two years of marriage. Respect and understanding are critical to a marriage. Everyone's journey is their own and for me, religion has paid only a small part in my life or my previous marriage. We choose which form of religion to embrace, but we have to remember that God loves all of His—or Her—children equally. Christian, Muslim or otherwise."

Khalil smiled and it was a beautiful sight to behold. "And you agree?" he asked Hassan.

"The major thing is respect," Hassan answered, stroking Blair's hand causing her to curl her fingers around his. "Since both of our religions are Abrahamic faiths, and originally were the same line of belief, they should be able to coexist. It is the cultures and fanatical foundations that impact religions and make them so disparate. When there's respect between the two people along all lines, then it will definitely work."

"There is but one God, though we may differ in how we worship, pray, and believe," Blair explained. "People have different levels of belief in the same household. Even within the same religion there are so many denominations. Believers and non-believers have stayed married for years. No different."

Khalil adjusted his tunic, then peered at her for a moment. "Explain what you mean."

"Back in Chicago, there are some women who go to church and their husbands stay home. Belief and spiritual endeavors are a personal thing with God." She paused, extracted her hand from Hassan's and took a sip of the bubbly liquid. "A few years ago, I read a novel about this very thing where the lead male character was a pastor and the First Lady assisted him in whatever he needed, but she did not believe in God. She was raised by strict COGIC parents but lost her faith after she became a victim of child sex trafficking. Their love helped them through everything, not their faith."

"I am fully aware of some real-world situations similar to what you read in the novel," Khalil said, his tone patient and empathetic. "But why does that story come to mind?"

"To be honest, I'm having a problem with my own faith," she confessed. "Especially given the climate in America right now. All of these religious people are trying to do such harm to women and to people of color. And since Christianity was not brought to us—Black people—in its pure form, the way Christ would have intended, I'm hard pressed to believe how Christianity can be the "only" path to God. It was used to enslave others merely as a means to distance us from our original path to God because money, greed, control, and lust were the prevailing factors. Not salvation."

She placed the wine glass on the table in front of her. "We are seeing a resurgence of that very 'Christian' spirit today in folks who believe Black people are unworthy, do not have souls, or bear any human consideration. And that women—even their own—are secondary to men's existence. This makes me so sad—and afraid for myself and what my children's future holds. That is one of the main reasons coming to Durabia was a good thing. I fear what living in America can do to them, only to find there's similar issues here in the Middle East."

Khalil nodded slowly, his face a mask of concern. "You both have given this a great deal of thought."

"We have talked about little else on the evenings we spend outside while the children are asleep," Hassan replied with an affectionate look at Blair. "So many things we have had to cover in such a short time since my father made it clear he is not pleased and is seeking to destroy what we have. I thought I would have time to court her, to let the children get to know me even more, for our families to accept the inevitable. My love for Blair is absolute."

Khalil waited for a moment, refilled Blair's glass then said, "The issues that divide marriages are money, religion, family, children. Right now, money is not the issue, and you seem to have covered the religion aspect. How are you going to deal with family in this regard? And another issue might come in when deciding what religion the children will embrace." He clasped both hands together. "If it is not both, and if one strongly believes one should be taught over the other, then that will also be a problem."

"We will deal with everything as it comes and I have no intention of putting the Sheikh in more of a precarious position than he's already in." Hassan looked into Blair's eyes and then back at Khalil. "So, to answer your question. Yes, our marriage can work. It means having mutual respect for the other and the understanding that there is truth in every religion, even if that truth is simply 'God is.'"

A smile creased Khalil's face. "That sounds about right. Now, let us figure out a way to deal with your father."

Chapter 12

Blair, still giddy from another wonderful dinner with Hassan, arrived at the front nurse's office and checked out what patients she'd been assigned for the day. She mentally calculated the equipment needed as she prepared for the first case coming her way.

She perched on the swiveling chair as she researched the patient's history, allergies, lab issues, and medications, then walked into the operating room and sent for the patient to be brought in. While she waited, she checked for implants, opening trays with instruments on display, including heavier ones for ortho procedures.

Blair completed the first count of instruments and soft goods that could become lost inside of a patient. She always tried to get this entire process done before the patient entered the room. The person undergoing surgery needed to be at ease, and the sound of instruments being tossed around could increase their anxiety. Blair took a few calming breaths of her own. Especially given an incident that happened yesterday.

Aniyah, a fellow surgical nurse, had followed Zaina's lead in taking an immediate dislike to Blair. This afternoon, after Blair had taken enough of Aniyah's crap, she had responded to a request by simply saying, "I'm on it."

Well, Blair must not have been Wal*Mart greeter cheerful enough because the woman lost her entire mind and went completely off in front of everyone. Even patients were disturbed by the scene. Blair didn't respond because all it would do at that point was add the wrong kind of fuel to the fire. Instead, she turned her back to the woman, ignoring her.

Somehow, that angered her more.

After the first surgery of the day, Blair was called into the director of nursing's office for a meeting with an HR representative. Blair stood in front of the desk because she didn't anticipate being there for long. She wasn't surprised to see that Aniyah was there too, looking like the cat that got the cream.

"It has been mentioned that other nurses are afraid of you," Salimah, the red-haired director of nursing said. "You intimidate them with what some of them call Black woman anger and sister-girl attitude."

Oh, so this is what they're on right now? Blair inhaled and let it out slowly, waiting. She couldn't do anything about anyone else's fear or perception, but that intimidation part was laughable. Blair did her job and did it well. That's what they hired her to do. Navigating everyone's icy vibes, and mistakes that they tried—unsuccessfully—to pin on her had become part of the process.

Then Salimah perched on the desk and said, "I need a promise from you that you'll tone down your attitude."

Blair thought that over for a minute and realized what they were looking for was a yes woman who would do things with no question without any pushback. And someone who would simply take everyone else's shit when she deserve it. They did not appreciate her confidence or knowledge.

"No." she said. "Considering that all I've done since day one was be the professional that this place hired me to be, I can't understand where this is coming from. Standing up for myself when my skills or decisions are questioned and doubted is good practice, not intimidation. So no, I don't know how others perceive me enough to know what they consider an 'attitude'."

She finally took a seat facing the two of them. "And since it's apparently so important to my position here that I'm arbitrarily aware of what it takes to please you and your friends, are you releasing me from my employment contract so I can go straight to my lawyer and figure this all out?" Blair adjusted her scrubs and crossed her legs. "I'm sure he can find out where two people who consider me to have an attitude factor into my employment here, while every doctor I've worked with can give me a sterling recommendation."

Aniyah's jaw nearly hit the floor. She shared a speaking glance with Salimah who bristled.

When they didn't respond, Blair checked her watch. "And you might want to call in my replacement fairly quickly since Dr. Earman's laminectomy begins in about fifteen minutes, and he'll need—"

"I mean, I ... I. No," Salimah stammered, inching backward.

Blair raised one brow. "No what?"

"That won't be necessary," she whispered, squirming.

"I'm confused," Blair said, pretending to scratch her head. "There are several issues on the table, so which part are you talking about?"

Salimah straightened her lapel. "No need for a lawyer or anything like that."

"Right." Blair stood, then glanced over her shoulder at Aniyah before she made it to the door. "You seem to take great pride in airing out my flaws in front of your friend and all the other nurses. I'd like for you to be just as verbal about things—in front of them—when you realize that you're wrong or when anyone else makes a mistake. That way, it won't seem so ... personal."

Both women flinched. *So much for tact.*

Blair was used to dealing with craziness and drama in her family, but she refused to allow it on the job, especially from people who held similar positions as hers. Doctors were another beast altogether. She expected it from them . . .

* * *

Though she'd been at Durabia Medical Hospital for the better part of a year, she was still new to the way this hospital did things and the learning curve was serious. Back home, it had taken about five years before she felt like an expert with handling the different cases, from vascular to orthopedic.

Once she managed to work with a spinal surgeon who had been through eight nurses. For this one surgery, she was responsible for cutting part of the bone, assembling the implant under the instruction of the medical representative who was present, passing instruments to the surgeon, and being an extra set of eyes and ears for the surgeon to make sure the procedure was progressing safely. That particular day, Blair also had to do the work of a missing part of the team since someone had called off at the last minute.

She understood last minute emergencies. As a parent and as a nurse, last minute was part of the job. But last minute became the norm, and suddenly the doctors were calling for Blair because they knew if no one else was available or knew how to manage their time wisely, she did. Word got around that some of the doctors were rescheduling their procedures to ensure that Blair was at their side when the time came. Also another bone of contention between the other nurses. But on this particular day, one surgeon disregarded her request to have someone to replace the missing staff member. Then he decided to show his entire ass and Blair had to hand it back to him on a platter . . .

"Look," she snapped after being given five sets of conflicting

instructions. "*I cannot cut bone, listen to the rep, and pass you instruments at the same time. I do not have three arms. You can either get another scrub nurse in here with me or I'm going to continue to work at my pace. Your call.*" *She looked the surgeon directly in his eyes, the only thing she could see above the scrubs and the mask.* "*I'm not going to speed things up when I'm not comfortable. If I drop an implant, guess what? We have to delay the case. Implants cost too much money to mess things up. The patient deserves better.*"

The only sounds in the room came from the suction machine, the heart monitor, and the music from The Artist Formerly Known as Prince playing in the background. Blair made sure her music was on before anyone entered the room and this surgeon didn't mind.

Five minutes after that, a second scrub nurse came to help.

When the next procedure started, that very same surgeon asked, "Are you all right, Blair? Are you ready to handle the next case?"

"Yes," she said, smiling as she used his words, "Let us begin."

The surgeon's assistant gave her the side eye and chuckled.

Unfortunately, the petty aggressions of Aniyah, Zaina, and Alia were a different sort of problem. Blair didn't think her medical expertise would solve things this time.

Black woman attitude? What in the entire hell?

Chapter 13

Dealing with the unnecessary drama from her co-workers was draining, but the satisfaction of taking care of patients was exhilarating. The main person who helped her balance everything was Hassan. He spent an extensive amount of time with Blair and the children. Sometimes he timed his work at the palace, so he could take her out to eat on lunch breaks. She never had to pay for anything, and everyone treated her like royalty, even when he wasn't with her. He respected her need for space, but she missed him when he wasn't around.

Their connection was strong and real. First as a friend, then growing to something more. It frightened her. She was so used to things going wrong, she couldn't be content when things were finally looking up. Like waiting for that next curve to be thrown instead of enjoying the pleasant parts of the moment. Hassan was different. The way he looked at her, listened to her, was so patient and encouraging that she felt calm and peaceful, and if she dared say—more beautiful when he was around. He was a dream come true; a distinct difference from the nightmare that she left behind in the States.

Since Durabia was the metropolis of the world, people from several cultures had settled there and Hassan had made sure to introduce her to different cuisines. He also educated her on the local customs to help her acclimate to the new culture.

As Blair and Hassan strolled along the path of the Durabian Cross River, other family drama was on her mind. One that started before she left Chicago and escalated the moment she settled into her new home.

Tiffany, one of her younger cousins, was in the hospital for a dislocated shoulder. Between her father's family history, and her nurse's training to be suspicious of children's injuries, Blair doubted the "slippery stairwell" story she was hearing from Dorsey. Not the first time this had happened. Either the youngsters in their family were totally uncoordinated and clumsy, or something was off. Blair definitely believed the latter.

She had already made her decision before the landline went dead. The rest of the children would have to come to Durabia. Blair knew new development might change things with Hassan, but sometimes one did whatever it took to protect those who could not protect themselves.

As they paused to take in the river view, she said, "I've petitioned for custody of three other kids, my younger cousins." Blair studied his face for a reaction as she explained the situation. He looked back at her with admiration written all over his face.

Hassan smiled at Blair, instantly putting her at ease. "They would be foolish not to grant your request. You can provide them with a great life."

"I'm confident I can, but Christian has agreed to help too. He's applied to take on two other children himself."

"Your cousin, right?"

She nodded as he mulled that over for a hot minute.

"They may need passports… paperwork. I will approach the embassy on your behalf if you like. Will you convert the gym into a bedroom?"

he asked as they continued along the winding path.

"I'm still working out the details." She squinted as she turned things over in her mind. How would this affect her home, her children? This were going so smoothly. Well, except Hassan's father who had campaigned the Durabian Tribunal to enact laws that would make it illegal for a member of the royal family to marry anyone outside of the family's approval. Sheikh Kamran was going up against the entire Muslim community and blocking that action.

Hassan laced his fingers with hers, drawing her attention. A wave of regret washed over her as she met his gaze. He'd already given her and her children so much. With the addition of more children, no man, no matter how understanding he was, could be expected to stick around. Why would he want to?

"Now I'll have even more relationship baggage than what I came here with."

"Children aren't baggage," Hassan protested. "They are blessings. But I do understand the difficulty of having a full household with your busy schedule. We are going to talk to Sheikh Kamran and Sheikha Ellena about this little dilemma. Maybe we can arrange for Christian and the other children to stay at the palace until we build this out to comfortably situate everyone."

Feeling more than a little relieved she said, "That sounds like a plan. At some point, I can arrange for Christian's mother to come stay with them as well. Being here with Christian would make her happy."

"Then it's settled," he said with a nod that signaled *and that's that*. "Children are like flowers; they thrive when they are surrounded by love and family."

Blair loved that Hassan always saw the positive in a situation. So many people would not get involved in such a sensitive family matter, but she couldn't do it. She couldn't leave those children to suffer the same fate as her aunts. Why did it seem that the women in their family attracted the same kind of men who damaged them when they were young?

"You're a remarkable woman, you know that" Hassan said, his voice filled with warmth. "My love, you have to trust me. Trust yourself."

"That's so hard," she confessed, gripping his hand tighter. "My biological father ... he never showed his face. My stepfather took on the role of father to me, but eventually he left too. Antonio didn't leave, but he also didn't do right by me or his children." She halted and looked up at him. "What if you leave me, too?"

Frowning, Hassan shook his head. "That will not be the case, my love."

"Your father will say otherwise."

"My father will not have a say in this." Hassan's voice carried such finality she didn't dare to disagree.

* * *

Blair and the children planned a morning brunch to surprise Fatimah. She made fresh scrambled eggs, lamb chops, and diced fruit while the kids whipped the batter for the pancakes. Blair had spoken with Fatimah the night before and asked that she come over for coffee. She wasn't expecting a big brunch, but it was the least they could do.

Blair wanted to subtly ask questions about the expectations for a woman who married into a royal family. She couldn't very well ask Auntie—correction—Sheikha Ellena, who was still navigating some aspects of her own marriage to Sheikh Kamran. Days would go by and no one would hear from her; still the aftermath of what had happened in Nadaum.

Fatimah had keys to the house since she was with the children the majority of the time while Blair was at work or picking up on-call shifts. While the oldest children were at school, Fatimah and the sunshine girl stayed on the move—seeing the sights of Durabia, taking walks in the park, and exploring some of the places the country had designated for children's development.

However, Blair was concerned with Fatimah's health. While she didn't complain or say anything, Blair knew she was not well. Fatimah's hand would stiffen up and shake whenever they sat down and had a conversation. But any mention of a doctor and Fatimah would shut her down.

"Good Morning," Fatimah said in that warm, cheery voice that seemed to brighten the atmosphere. Her footsteps were light as she made her way down the hallway and into the open kitchen and dining room area.

The children left their little stations and took off running to greet her the same way they did their American grandmother. Although Fatimah was with them most of the time, they were as excited to see her as if it had been months. She was a Godsend, such a breath of fresh air.

Fatimah had been a little tense around Blair at first, but the children had warmed her a great deal. Sometimes, it even seemed as though she was encouraging Hassan and Blair to be together. Fatimah had grown up in the era of obligation. She wanted more for her sons; wanted them to have a choice. "The world is changing," she said one day while the sunshine girl was stretched out on her lap. "My sons will have happier lives. They will know what love is."

"Teta. Teta," the children yelled, using the Arabic name for grandmother.

She hugged them to her bosom, and her eyes widened at the sight of all the food. "Oh, my goodness," she said in her thickly accented English. "What is all of this?"

Blair laughed. "Yes, Mrs. Khan. There is coffee and some other good things. Have a seat and relax. You take care of us all the time, today we're going to take care of you. Brandon will get you some coffee."

Brandon was always helpful. He seemed to bask in the attention from Hassan, Fatimah, and the Kings the most. The Kings, Knights and Hassan were definitely the positive male influence that he needed. And her girls watched them, taking in how they treated the women. Hopefully, Bella and Lola would never endure the type of experiences she had in relationships. The transition from America to Durabia had been fairly easy because both Hassan and Fatimah went out of their way to make sure Blair and the children had everything they needed. Coming from a family that was part drama and part insane, with only a few key members having any common sense, these two additions to her family along with their extended family were so important. Even Hassan's brothers Akeem and Haleem were good to her and the children. Where was this kind of love when she was growing up? Her mother could definitely have used this kind of support. Maybe Blair would not have ended up with someone like Antonio. Maybe.

"We are incredibly grateful to have you around," Blair said, sliding a plate in front of Fatimah. "I'm grateful that you have made things so easy. You have shown us complete love, acceptance, and understanding. More than I expected from anyone here."

Fatimah settled Lola into the seat next to hers. "This is so kind of you all. I am happy to help out any time. I love to be around young people, and your children bring great joy to my heart. And please do not hesitate to call me for anything." She inhaled and smiled before scanning the counter. "This food smells wonderful. The children did all of this?"

"We did the pancakes," Brandon said. "Mom did everything else."

"I helped," Bella chimed in.

Fatimah beamed at Brandon before taking Lola and Bella's hand and said, "Let's say our grace."

Once the meal was underway, Fatimah said, "Blair, it is very obvious that my son is smitten with you. I'd like to know your intentions in regards to Hassan."

Blair nearly choked on a forkful of eggs. Well so much for her kicking off the conversation.

* * *

Blair walked into the house after a graveyard shift. She had almost made it out of the hospital when she was paged for an emergency in the OR.

"Blair, where were you?" Hassan asked in a voice so panicked that a shiver alarm shot through her.

"Why, what's going on." She scanned the living room and found her children sitting on the sofa instead of being in bed where they belonged. Was it his mother? "What's wrong? Why are they still down here?"

His jaw was set when he said, "You didn't tell me you were going to be late."

"Hassan, calm down. I was pulled into a surgery right as I hit the exit. There was no time to call." She peered around him at Brandon who had a worried expression. Bella and Lola were asleep, snuggled against him. "And that doesn't explain why they're still downstairs up past their bedtime."

"My mother isn't here."

"And you can't put them to bed?" she asked, glaring at him and sighing with a weariness she felt all the way down to her toes.

"You don't understand—"

"No, I understand completely," she snapped. "Another man who feels certain things are women's work, huh?"

"Blair," he said, in a warning tone. "I never put the children to bed. I have never been in their bedrooms or bathrooms since you moved here."

"What the hell is wrong with you?" she snapped.

"I never—" he inhaled sharply, and his chest heaved with his frustration. "I am never alone with the children. Ever. I don't give them baths, tuck them in, or anything like that."

Blair blinked several times absorbing that information, trying to process what that could mean. Out of the corners of her eyes, she watched Brandon wake and escort his sisters up the stairs.

"I never want you to question that my love for you—and for the children—is anything but pure," he whispered. "Any little action, or sign of affection can be construed as the wrong thing."

Realization slammed into her. The times that The Sunshine Girl tried to climb on his lap and he quickly settled her in the seat beside him. And Brandon, who always wanted to embrace Hassan, who immediately put out his fist for a "pound" instead. Making sure that all three of the children were always together—at all times when he was present. And no, he didn't venture upstairs any longer. Even his sleeping quarters were now in the solarium and not in the guest bedroom he'd made into his own before she arrived. All of it, every action, designed to elicit her trust—the one thing she did not have in spades.

Blair's legs went weak and she lost the ability to support her weight. Then, her eyes flooded.

Hassan caught her before she landed on the floor and gathered her in his arms as she sobbed.

"I never want you to doubt me," Hassan whispered against her hair.

Finally, she pulled away to look into his eyes, her vision blurred by tears. This man was a treasure, with boundless love for her and her children. "To be honest, I didn't realize I should doubt you. Safe is the only thing that I've ever felt with you. They feel it too."

Whatever guard she had on her heart slipped into oblivion. No, it wasn't flowers, candy, or dinners that were tokens of affection—it was a man who cared about the things that mattered most.

Chapter 14

"Jai, I'd like your thoughts on something," Blair said, the minute his assistant led her into his office, where he sat behind a computer screen at an ornate, black corner desk with metal legs. Near the window, a black shelf was filled with medical books ranging from Western to Eastern practices. On the top shelf, a range of framed degrees announced Jai's skill in different forms of medical science and holistic modalities.

Jaidev Maharaj, King of Devon and a medical doctor with experience managing a facility in the states, towered over her by several inches, and had a shock of silver at the widow's peak of his dark, silky hair that was much like his father Khalil.

"Shoot," he said, placing a folder to one side of the desk and giving her his full attention.

She took a seat and handed him a set of documents. "Durabia has all sorts of medical centers that focus on *physical* healing. Not a lot of them deal with the mental and emotional recovery that women and children need to fully overcome trauma from sexual and physical abuse or neglect."

Jai paused for a moment. "That's a good observation. Especially given the fact that Dubai is right next-door and women who have been lured into sex trafficking come here to Durabia when they escape that cycle. Sheikha Ellena's center provides assistance to those women, and ones who were from El Zalaam, as needed. The Sheikh's family was none too happy. Now that they're out of the picture, Kamran is having a hell of a time shutting that place down. The Tribunal is not hearing it."

Blair tapped the proposal in front of him. "We need to find a way to help those women."

"Why the sudden interest?"

As he scanned the pages, Blair shared a little of her family history. Jai tried to keep a straight face at some of the tragic things that befell her family members. Some of it mirrored what Temple experienced in her young life and during the twelve months she had been in a coma and wound up pregnant at one of Jai's facilities.

"I brought it to the attention of the doctors at Durabia Medical Hospital," Blair said. "They said if I could raise the money for a facility, they would do the legwork to get one built."

"Very proactive," he mused with a smile and looked so much like his father, Khalil, that she almost gasped.

"Yes, but I don't think they're taking me seriously at all."

"They will when you return with this." Jai pulled out a sheet of paper from the desk drawer, grabbed a pen and created a chart. He put his name on the first line, along with an amount. He passed the handwritten sheet to her and said, "Go to each one of the Kings, then the Knights. Show them this small business plan as it perfectly outlines the premise and the purpose, and they'll each contribute to the funding. Then go back and have a conversation with the hospital officials you've been talking to. They will take you seriously when they see there's money on the table." He scanned her proposal again. "Then again, with this much support, you might want to consider going out on your own. Just a thought."

Blair left the office with a new pep in her steps and determination in her spirit.

Since Hassan had encouraged her to use her royal status to become a sponsor of several businesses, soon she would be able to work because she *wanted* to, not because she *had* to. Once, Hassan had made a light-hearted joke that Blair would have to make a lot of money for their sunshine girl to live in style. Truthfully, he was always the one who indulged her children, but he did it in such a way that it didn't seem like spoiling. His encouragement and attentiveness to Brandon and Bella as they showed him their progress reports or gave him status updates on their current school projects reinforced their good behavior. Blair's youngest had taken to Hassan as if he was her father. Seeing the two of them together brought her such joy. Brandon tried to emulate Hassan as much as possible, the same way he had done with Christian. They were the only two positive male influences in his life before the Kings and Knights came onto the scene. Now there was an overload of their type in her life. She was being influenced as well.

* * *

"So, you're still making payments on the mortgage, right?" Antonio said. His bitter tone carried across the thousands of miles. "You know, until the sale of the house goes through and all that."

Saltwater rushed into her mouth. Twelve months felt like twelve minutes as her head flooded with images of broken bones and bloody smiles for Blair, all at the hands of a man who promised before God and everyone to love her … honor her. Cherish her.

Blair tried to hold onto her temper as she walked into the living room with the phone to her ear. "Yes, because you might not care about your credit rating, but I care about mine. Taking care of a grown ass man was not part of my plans, but since you don't know how to make payments on time, I have to cover my own ass."

"Good, then I can go ahead and get this new car."

Blair closed her eyes and tried not to scream. His need to punish her for not accepting his bull was epic. New car? Was he not aware that having a roof over one's head was the most important thing?

"Why can't you get Netty to do the honors, since she's next in line to be your Splenda Mama, since she can't afford to be a full-out Sugar Mama?"

"I don't need my mama, Netty, or any woman," he shot back, and had the nerve to sound offended, probably more about that Splenda Mama quip because Netty's struggles were real. "I'm doing good on my own."

"It's not on your own if I'm footing the bill," she countered, dripping down onto the sofa and punching the nearest cushion. "You're just pissed that I decided not to hang with you during your 'struggle to be great', as you call it. The only thing you're great at is pimping wallets. And now that those other children have surfaced, the court is going to make you pay child support and cover medical insurance for them, too." Blair made a mental note to return a call to Jai about the additional children who would be in her care. "Enjoy this little bit of free time, because the minute that house is sold, you're going to have to find some balls and man up."

"Come on bae, don't be like that," he whined, sounding absolutely pitiful and a tad bit drunk. "I'm only going to have half a grand to live off if the court takes over."

Blair dropped on the sofa, rubbing her forehead. "Well, maybe you should have thought of that before you created three whole new children while you were married. Then you had the nerve to want to put that thing in me. Whew! I'm so glad I started shutting that down years ago.

I didn't even know you were doing any other dirt besides Netty, but my body must've known your community peen was tainted."

"Oh, that's cold," he mumbled.

True, it could be considered a low blow, but it was truth. And she had finally tired of holding on to her marriage just for the children's sake. This relationship had been the mother of all relationship lessons. She couldn't remember what made her fall for him but looking in the rearview mirror she should have kept on driving or backed up over him a couple of times. Maybe three time.

Rolling her eyes toward the ceiling, she added, "Thank God for Auntie Amanda."

"That meddling bi—"

"Careful, Antonio," she snapped. "Life and death are said to be in the power of the tongue, and honey, you're on life support."

"Yeah, I'm not gonna be your life support. Since you got it like that. You can count me out on the child support thing."

"Like that's something new."

Auntie Amanda had always warned that Blair needed to start looking out for number one. *"You're a grown ass woman with four children,"* she had said. *"Act like it. Stop watering a dead plant. Lose that weed and move on. You deserve the peace and happiness you strive to give everyone else."*

Blair stopped washing dishes to process that statement. "Auntie, I only have three children."

"Four, because that includes him," she countered. *"He's trying to talk you into buying a bigger house when you're already covering all the bills because he's so irresponsible with his money. Why do that to yourself? Cut that fool loose and do it on your own."* Amanda shook her head and took another shot of Amaretto. *"He's only hanging on to you because he wants your income to take care of all those extra children*

when he didn't have the decency to put a muzzle on that thing to protect you or himself." She folded her arms over her breasts. "That man can kick pebbles because rocks are too strong for him. Let. Him. Go."

Blair's Grandma Ruth had been the one to say that having a piece of man was better than having no man at all. Blair could only thank God for mamas and aunties, because Ellena, Amanda, and Melissa had always delivered their wisdom straight, with no chaser—leave him.

"To hell with what anyone else was saying about sticking it out in a bad marriage. You're in that damn marriage by yourself," Auntie Amanda continued. "Don't carry his burdens and let him suck up all of your good years while you're trying to prove what a good wife you are to a man who has been a husband in name only." She nodded as she considered the advice dished to her over the years. "Let him bear his own burdens. Let him take care of his own responsibilities without your income being a factor. Let your best friend have him all to herself and she can be the one to take your place."

And so she did.

When Blair made the break, the first thing out of his mouth was that she was one of those weak women who couldn't hold a brother down.

First of all, he was no "brother". He was half Mexican and half Black. Second, Auntie Amanda was more than right—she couldn't afford to take care of a grown ass man and provide well enough for her three children, too—along with his unexpected additions to the tribe.

Antonio had a "nose" and clothes habit that would put even the richest woman in the poor house. When Blair finally shut off the financial tap and changed the security information on all of her accounts, Netty had to step up to the plate. Netty didn't realize that Antonio would only keep her around for as long as she was making enough money to do what he needed. The minute she showed signs of failing, he was going to leave her drained and financially dry. That was his M.O. The managerial jobs at several furniture rental places only lasted about as long as his patience did. After the first or second paycheck, the trial always ended with a confrontation and some diatribe about how "the man" was keeping him down or his boss thought he was better than him.

Strangely enough, he did manage to talk Netty into getting a bigger apartment so his outside children could visit, and she could help take care of them, but Blair doubted he was making much of a contribution to that household. The last time Blair laid eyes on her best friend, she looked tore down from the floor down and needed a checkup from the neck up. The mistress had aged a good fifteen years in just twelve months. Drinking all that liquor and stealing someone's husband could do that, as well as doing what was necessary to keep him. Word on the street was that he had already lined up her replacement.

Was it worth it, Netty?

The words burned on her lips as she watched her old friend at the grocery store a month before leaving for Durabia, putting basic things to the side at the cash register to avoid an over ring. Netty hurried from the building with two small bags and what little dignity she had left. Blair paid for the discarded groceries, rushed out behind her old friend and put them on the car, the steered the cart to her own vehicle. Just as was ready to pull off, Netty knocked on the window. Blair lowered it enough to look at her friend.

"I'm not sorry, Blair," she said. "I know that's what you think I should say, but I'm not. As for the groceries—"

"It's fine Netty. Live and be happy."

"I'll pay you back," she whispered, and shame radiated from her. "Every cent...."

Blair studied her friend for a long time then smiled. "No thanks. Last time you did that you lost a friend. I certainly didn't."

Blair shuddered before she blinked away the memory, turned the ignition and made her way home.

She quickly disconnected the call with Antonio cutting off the full volume of his wrath.

Then took in a cleansing breath as she stepped out onto the patio. The sunshine girl and Fatimah were playing a rousing game of Patti Cake. Off to her left in the shade, her eldest children Brandon and Bella were involved in a game of Bid whist with Hassan looking on. He waved at her

"Blair, you must save me," Hassan said faking a panicked expression. "Brandon and Bella have hoodwinked me into this game for Michigan cherries and I am tapped." Blair eyed the bag of the chewy red candy sitting on the table and the fact a mountain was on the children's side, and only a few pieces were on his. Hassan knew full well how to play the game and her children were still learning. Blair laughed so hard she was in tears.

The sun warming her face confirmed the peace settling in her spirit. She was done. Totally done. She would call her lawyer's office in the morning. Antonio could have the house and whatever else was left behind. Blair's life, her future and all that she had dreamed of stretched out before her. She snagged the bag of sweet red treats and waved them in Hassan's direction.

"Help is on the way."

Chapter 15

"Olivia has a brain tumor," Jessica said when Blair answered the call that came as she was going on break.

She had been doing her best to distance herself from anything or anyone related to her soon to be ex-husband. As much as she didn't want to have this conversation personally, Blair was a nurse and took pride in her chosen profession. Besides, Olivia wasn't a terrible person like her narcissistic son.

Blair's sister-in-law was an interesting person to deal with from day one. At first, she sided with her brother on their marital issues. Then, after being a witness to him losing his mind on that night when he dragged Blair out of the house, she did a one-eighty and tried to knock some sense into him. Jessica was a pint-size ball of fire with red hair and blue contacts that contrasted her creamy complexion. After everything she'd been through, with a husband who left her before their child made it into this world, she didn't take anyone's mess—not even her brother's.

"They want to operate," Jessica explained. "But I'm not feeling the hospital where they're trying to send her to have the surgery done."

"Where is it?" Blair asked, sliding out her last surgeon preference card and tossing it into the bin.

"Cook County."

Blair sighed as realization dawned. "Cook County gets a bad rap, but it's a damn good hospital, Jess. It's also a training ground for doctors who are just starting out and a teaching one for seasoned physicians as well."

"You're in the medical field," Jessica protested. "Can't you get her to a place where she'll have the top doctors? This is my mama we're talking about."

After that incident, Olivia had always been there for Blair when she needed her. She had the key to Blair's house, often picked up the kids from school, and would cook for them sometimes. She knew what it felt like to raise three kids with a husband who wasn't an active part of their lives. Olivia was the main reason Blair was able to complete the different phases of her education and enter the medical field. She owed the woman a great deal.

"I'll see what I can do," Blair said to Jessica. "But I don't have any pull in Chicago."

Jessica sighed loud enough for Blair to hear the frustration. "But it doesn't have to be here. I said, 'I want the *best*'."

Blair slowed her steps. Hassan was waiting for her beside his car, concern etched on his face. "What does that mean, Jess?"

Silence.

"You mean here? In Durabia?"

"Well, you've got a lot more pull there and I've read a lot of great things about that place. They have the best doctors in the world. Come on, Blair. You know how they treat folks on Medicare over here. Even folks on HMO's don't get a fair shake."

* * *

Briefly pulling the phone from her ear, Blair quickly processed what Jess was asking of her. How could she honestly open the door for Antonio to make an excuse to travel to Durabia? Her protective nature kicked in. She didn't want to get involved, but she couldn't live with herself if something happened to Olivia.

"I'll look into it. I'll have Jai Maharaj coordinate with you to get her records."

"Thank you so much," she said, breathing a sigh of relief. "You know, even though my brother is an asshole, and he tried to make everything seem your fault, I've always liked you."

"You're just saying that because you need me," Blair said, hastening her steps to make it to Hassan.

Jessica gasped. "Busted, but it's true. You were always too good for him. He never grew up. Too much easy money and indulgence, and not enough common sense," she said with a calm voice. "Thank you for helping me; for helping *us*."

Blair didn't want to offer any excuses. Family came first. Olivia and Jessica were still her relatives by marriage. She couldn't use Antonio as the reason to avoid doing the right thing. "I'll call you when I have news. Jess, these arrangements are just going to be for you and Olivia. Your brother does not have an open invitation to travel here. Do you understand that?"

"I understand Blair. This isn't about my brother, just making sure that *mi madre* gets the best care so that she can be here with us a lot longer. I promise Antonio won't be an issue."

Taking a deep breath before reaching the car, Blair pasted on a smile. That unexpected call shook her up a bit, but she wouldn't allow it to ruin the rest of her evening. A handsome man awaited for her a few steps away.

Hassan held her door open and said, "The sunshine girl wants to go to Enchanted Planet tonight."

The Enchanted Planet was a family entertainment center not too far from Durabia Mall.

Blair waited until he slid behind the wheel to say, "Does she now?"

"Yes, she used her phone to take a picture of the commercial and showed it to me," Hassan said, chuckling.

"Genius."

"Like her mother." He gave her an appreciative glance before focusing on the road.

"Hmm, flattery will get you everywhere." Blair settled in the passenger seat as a warm sensation rolled through her body.

"Everywhere or everything?"

"Both." Blair took in his sexy profile and the edges of her mouth curled up. "Let's get in a little adult time *after* the children have their fun."

"Sounds like a plan."

Adult time was all about music, movies, and talking about the things that moved them—desires, hopes, and dreams. Being with a man with no sexual expectations had been refreshing. Hassan certainly held to his religious restrictions of being married before they took that next step in their relationship. Even though her Auntie Amanda was encouraging her to take him for a "sexual test drive" before any type of marriage. She had made that mistake in her own marriage and landed a man who didn't know how to parallel park, do a one-eighty turn, or even put his "car" in drive, reverse, or neutral. Blair had laughed at her aunt's blunt talk, but that was still one thing she wouldn't do—press for something that Hassan's religion was totally again. No matter how much she wanted him. He was treating her with the same respect as a single woman of his culture, despite the fact that she already had children and had been married.

Blair would share the news about Olivia with Hassan later in the evening. Right now, she wanted to enjoy their time together. No thoughts about the hospital or the fact that her marriage to Antonio was the gift that keeps on giving.

* * *

A few days later, Jai contacted Blair and had her come in with Hassan to discuss options for Olivia. "She shouldn't be flying in her condition," he explained. "If we do it, we might have to put her in a coma before flying her out. It's a risk and I wouldn't recommend it."

"Do you think we should use a private yacht instead?" Hassan suggested, shifting in the chair across from Jai's desk. "It should take about three or four days to get her here from overseas."

"Overseas?" Blair croaked, remembering that motion sickness had sidelined Olivia for the first part of the honeymoon cruise she took with Blair and Antonio.

"That definitely sounds like a better alternative," Hassan said, giving her hand a gentle pat. "I will have it arranged. Do not worry."

"Thank you."

Hassan waited until he dropped Blair off at the hospital, gave her a kiss and was out of earshot to make another call to Sheikh Kamran. "Uncle, how do I go about purchasing a yacht?"

Chapter 16

Seven days later, on a Monday, Blair was halfway through a long eight-hour day. All the cases were going smoothly as scheduled, when Aniyah burst into the sub sterile room where Blair was getting supplies. "Blair, you need to come with me."

"She's in the middle of circulating," said Janii, the tall brunette surgical tech that was helping Blair.

A circulating registered nurse did the preparation for an operation, and then continually monitored the patient and staff during its course.

"Dr. Ahmad Maharaj requested her for a pseudo-aneurysm," Aniyah said as all eyes went to her. "He has to do an emergency vascular case in room nine."

Blair gave the surgeon an apologetic look and said, "Dr. Rajoub, the other nurse can help you with the rest of this case."

Before he could object, she followed the woman down the hall, past the nurse's station and asked, "So, what are we working with?"

Aniyah handed Blair the chart. "The patient is a male, thirty-eight years old. He had a pseudoaneurysm in his leg."

Which meant "false" aneurysm—a collection of blood that formed between the two outer layers of an artery. Something that shouldn't require Blair's presence.

"The patient experienced a complication during cardiac catheterization."

Blair realized this would be a tough one. The procedure, in which a thin, flexible tube—a catheter—is inserted into the femoral artery at the groin and threaded through blood vessels up to the heart, could be complex.

"He came from the cath lab," Aniyah said, circling around the team of vascular doctors on the way to the door. "And they couldn't control bleeding in the femoral artery."

"So, we need to put a stitch in his thigh to stop the bleeding?"

"Pretty much," she replied, keeping pace with Blair.

"So why couldn't you do it?"

Aniyah narrowed her eyes and clenched her lips before replying, "The surgical team specifically requested you."

The team was prepped and ready to go.

Unfortunately, as soon as Dr. Maharaj opened the patient up, blood gushed from his leg. "Shit," the surgeon yelled out, then followed with a string of profanity.

Not the best sign. Blair had learned to outwardly stay calm in stressful situations, but panic was doing a deathly tango in her mind. She placed some lap sponges in the surgical area to hold pressure while the surgeon tried to work out his next move. He let loose with another string of curses because he couldn't see where the bleeding originated. Blair inhaled and remained silent. The suction canister held several units of blood—that was a massive loss.

The scrub nurse held pressure to the artery with a bunch of surgical towels while Blair suctioned the area so that Dr. Maharaj could get a clearer view. When he still couldn't find the source of the bleeding, Blair screamed, "Damn!" and it mirrored everyone's sentiment. She might have to do CPR because if the patient died, they were all in trouble. Lawsuits would come from everywhere.

Finally, Dr. Maharaj spotted the issue, cleared an area, and they were able to control the bleeding. They also had to give the patient several units of blood during the procedure because he was losing so much.

"Glory to God," Blair whispered when it seemed the patient was in the clear. Everyone laughed, including the surgeon.

"How are you cursing with the same mouth you're using to speak praises?" Dr. Maharaj said with a chuckle.

"Well, you cursed first, then you were probably thanking God, too," she shot back, grinning.

The surgeon gave her a sheepish smile as he chuckled. "True."

* * *

Blair had been pulled into yet another surgery just before it was time to leave. Now that she was finally home, she was too tired to even think about cooking or cleaning. Thanks to Hassan and Fatimah, she never had to worry about the children when she was working, or when they had late night plans. The invites for Blair and Hassan to attend events had ramped up ever since that night on the yacht. Blair now had a social life to go along with family and work life, and something about having all three made her feel a little overwhelmed.

Tonight, when she stepped over the threshold, a sudden emptiness hit her. No sounds, except from in the kitchen. But the feel was ... off. She realized that the children weren't there even without going to their rooms to check.

Stepping a few more feet into the living room, she was greeted by candles and flowers that had been strategically placed throughout, leading all the way to the dining room. The place was spotless, no toys, no clothes—and she was grateful that someone else had done the honors.

Blair kept moving until she could find the explanation for all this unexpected beauty unfolding before her. The scent of cumin hit, and she followed it to the kitchen where Hassan was at the stove, plating a meal of basmati rice, stuffed chicken, grilled asparagus, garlic pita, and salad. All of it smelled so good, her stomach did a tango and almost made it to the table before she did.

Watching him prepare their meal with such finesse made her heart sing. No man, except Hassan, had ever done this for her. No man had cared enough to ensure that after a long day she had a decent meal prepared by his own hands. This was different. And so very appreciated.

He held out the chair for her to take a seat opposite from him, then whipped the napkin from the table, spread the fabric, and placed it on her lap when she settled in.

"Full service, huh?" she asked, as he slid the jacket from her shoulders then extracted a small hot towel from a bowl in front of him and cleansed her hands.

"Nothing but the best." Hassan's gaze shone with affection. "My mother made sure the men in her family could appreciate what it took to make a good meal," he answered, sliding into his seat, and pouring her a glass of sparkling grape juice.

He remembered, no alcoholic beverages during the work week. Even his choice of music was awesome. Smooth jazz played in the background as they exchanged small talk. When she tried to shift the conversation to questions about him, he deflected and said, "Tonight is all about you."

They chatted about several sites she still hadn't visited and when they could go.

When she finished the meal, Hassan extended his hand and switched the music selection to *Adore* by Prince before leading her out to the patio to dance under the moonlight.

They were comfortable with each other, despite the rocky beginning. Nothing she did or said met with judgment, good or bad. Even opposing views were accepted with appreciation. Agreeing to disagree, but respecting each point was so refreshing.

Hassan Ali Khan was becoming someone she didn't want to do without.

Chapter 17

Fatimah had called Hassan earlier that morning to inform him that his father desired an audience. Hassan had been waiting for this conversation. His father continually expressed displeasure at how much time Hassan spent with Blair. Over the past week, he had ramped up his arguments to the point Hassan thought the man would have a heart attack.

He pulled his Rolls Royce into the seven-car garage and entered the home through the kitchen so he could greet his mother first. Fatimah's dark-brown eyes were filled with worry. He hated putting her in the unfortunate position of doing anything against his father's wishes. She loved Blair and the children and insisted on caring for them herself instead of having them go to a center before or after school. Every day that Blair attempted to separate them, his mother insisted it was too soon. He had never seen his mother so happy than when teaching the children things that would make their life in Durabia that much easier.

"Have a seat, son. There is something we need to discuss," Yousef said to Hassan the moment he entered the office with a view of the main palace.

Hassan exhaled as he settled in the space opposite his father on the plush cushions of the couch, fully prepared to do battle.

Yousef's hard glare would normally send a little fear into any adversary's heart. Not today. Hassan could only hope his father would relent. But the man's stubbornness was legendary. If Yousef chose to withdraw his support, Hassan had been secretly amassing his own fortune so he wouldn't need anything from him. He couldn't hope to guide Blair in her financial life and not take his own advice.

"I know what you are going to say, father, because you have already said it more than once. In fact, almost twice a day now. So, I need to ask, is your desire that I not marry her because she is Black or because she is not Durabian?"

Yousef's confused expression was interesting given the fact that both were true. He was trying to pick the answer he deemed less offensive.

"You are my son and I love you dearly, but if you marry that woman—whose womb has already been spoiled three times, I will revoke my title and my position as your father. I do not want any part of your union with her. I will not attend your wedding. I will not attend your funeral. I will no longer be an existence in your life. Of course, you will no longer exist in mine."

Fatimah, overhearing the conversation between her son and husband, rushed from the kitchen into the living room. "Yousef, why are you crying wolf to our son with your threats? Are you thinking clearly and rationally to be sure this is the only option? Are you even prepared to walk away from this situation?"

"Mama," Hassan said, leaving his seat to stand by her side. "It is going to be all right. I will be all right."

"I have something to say now, son," she shot back. "Let me speak."

Turning her gaze back to her husband, she continued, "Blair Swanson is a good woman, Yousef, regardless of her race, her complexion, her nationality. She is a good person for our son. He loves her and she loves him, I have seen the way they look at each other." Her hands balled into fists by her side. "Why do we have to abide by the laws? We should abide by love, abide by hope and compassion. Our son should not have to tolerate and suffer in a world where he is not happy."

Yousef stood, anger etched in his face. "Stand down, woman! This conversation is between me and my son."

"No, you have a seat, man," she countered, her tunic rustling with the sharp movements that carried her closer. "So many families are broken today because of situations like this. I want to be a part of Blair and those beautiful children's lives. I also want our son to have children of his own with Blair, inshallah. We should be a family of heart and love, not a family of hate and division." Fatimah moved until she stood inches from her husband. "What is the alternative, Yousef? Do you have a next plan? What if your other sons decide they want to marry someone they are actually in love with? Are you going to disown them as well? What if they decide to end their relationship with you because you want to end your relationship with Hassan? Have you thought about that?"

Yousef swayed on his feet. "I … I … I … I"

"No, this is too detrimental to my heart," she cried, gripping his dishdasha. "I will not be able to forgive you if you decide not to be a part of our son's life. I do not want to be in your life if this is the direction you are heading with our children."

Yousef's face turned a bright shade of crimson as he stared into his wife's eyes. "Are you threatening me?"

Fatima moved around him but smiled thinly over her shoulder. "You are threatening my son. So, while you are wasting time on revenge, remember to be prepared to face your own karma since you are trying so hard to hurt others. Especially your own flesh and blood."

When Hassan realized his mother was done throwing down her gauntlet, he spoke up. "Father, I will not be swayed by your opinion about my future wife. I do love you father, but I am deeply in love with Blair Swanson and I am going to marry her. This will be a life-altering position for both of us." Hassan went to his mother, who was close to sobbing, and gathered her in his arms. "Mother, thank you for loving me for me and accepting my decision to be with the woman I love, and the children. *My* children."

He locked gazes with his angry father. "If there are consequences, we will deal with them accordingly. We will weather this storm with or without you in our lives, Father, and the lives of our children and children yet to come. One thing I have learned from this experience is that I will be a great husband and father. I will love my children unconditionally and support the decisions that they make in their lives and allow them to learn their own lessons. We will be a family of love, honor, and respect."

Yousef dropped into his seat, his disdain evident in the tense set of his shoulders and his sour expression. He glared at his wife. "That marriage is not going to happen, not as long as I'm alive."

Tears streamed down Fatimah's face as she asked, "What are you going to do? You have already caused so much damage."

Hassan kissed his mother on the cheek and walked out of the room to pack up the last of his belongings.

Still weeping, Fatimah made her exit, placing a hand to her heart saying a prayer in Arabic.

Several minutes later Hassan came back down, embraced his mother, headed towards the door with two of the servants and his brothers helping to carry the rest of his things.

Yousef stood up from one of the sofas and said, "I will give my blessing under one condition."

Hassan froze. So did Fatimah and his siblings. They all slowly turned to face him.

"You have to marry her within one month from this day to keep your inheritance, property, and place in the hierarchy of rulership. Failing that, you must keep your betrothals to the women you were originally scheduled to marry."

One month. They could manage that. *Easily*.

Chapter 18

Olivia Perez's brain surgery was done in Durabia, but her recovery was far from easy. She had been a diva all her life, so her hospital room was accented and decorated to feel more like a five-star hotel.

Her walk was slow and tortuous, but she did it while smiling and making it to her destination. After a week, she gained enough strength to walk without the assistance of any devices. The nurses offered her a wheelchair, but she refused.

Her speech was slurred, but she could be understood. She remained in the hospital for two weeks post-surgery and endured three weeks of extensive rehabilitation after that, with physical, occupational, and speech therapy.

Blair was on full rotation at work and could only see to Olivia's care in her free moments. Jessica had made the trip from Chicago as well, and was with her mother at all times. Though it was painful seeing her struggle to relearn to use her right side and how to speak again, Blair admired her strength and determination.

Her words took longer to enunciate but Olivia was able to walk, talk, and even, with Jessica riding shotgun, drive herself short distances within months. She still had a few more aneurysms in her brain, which had to be removed. But the surgeon said her brain needed to heal completely from their first efforts before going back in for another surgery.

Throughout this entire experience, Antonio kept reaching out to Jessica under the guise of worry for Olivia. She only gave him a minimal amount of her time, because their mother's health was her main focus. Soon, she had no choice but to limit her conversations with him by cutting him off the minute he started drilling her about Blair. Not the children – *Blair*. He had been leaving harsh and menacing threats on Blair's voicemail about his mother and the inability to see his children. He even called the palace and harassed the staff trying to get to Sheikha Ellena.

Blair had put Hassan on notice that Antonio had made attempts to travel to Durabia. If he did manage to come, she didn't want him anywhere near her or his mother until she healed completely.

Hassan promised to take care of her request.

Blair made it to the rehab center of hospital a little early, wanting to check in on Olivia before beginning her shift. She was smiling from ear to ear because joyful thoughts of Hassan filled her mind. But just as she was reaching for the door handle of Olivia's room, she could feel a warm breath on the back of her neck.

"Hi honey, you miss me?"

Blair whipped around at the familiar and unwelcome voice. She couldn't believe she was looking in Antonio's face. *Did Jessica betray my trust and invite him here?*

"What are you doing here?" she asked, clearly shaken by this unexpected visitor. Hassan had taken steps to block his entry, and for Antonio to bypass that mean he was already here.

"My mama's in that room, right?"

"Yes, but you aren't supposed to be here."

He grabbed her arm and moved her away from the door, into an empty hospital room nearby. She remained calm the whole time, contemplating her next move. Knowing how volatile he could be at the drop of a dime; Blair didn't want to say or do anything to set him off. But thanks to Khalil, who insisted that she, like her aunt Ellena, take self-defense training from the Kings; she could actually "put in *that work*" and whip his entire ass. But doing so on hospital grounds could cost her position since his mother was a patient.

"Are you here to check on your mother?" she asked, stepping back slightly.

"Of course I'm here to see her, but I also came to see *my wife* and children."

Blair chuckled, shaking her head. "Your what?" *This man has lost his mind.*

"Nothing is funny Blair. You are *still* my wife," he said with a slight edge to his voice.

As she looked at the man in front of her, Blair couldn't believe that she'd ever became so deeply involved with him. *When you think you're in love, you can make some crazy decisions.* Antonio was definitely one of those, although she was thankful for her children.

Antonio closed the gap that she'd created and pushed her up against one of the walls. He licked his lips, preparing to lean forward and provide an unwanted kiss. He was there one minute, and in the blink of an eye he was removed from her space.

"Hassan!" *Where the hell did he come from?*

And he wasn't alone. Three muscular men, who resembled highly skilled secret service agents, bore down on him. Two of them had Antonio immobilized, while Hassan walked over to Blair. He took her in his arms and kissed her forehead. She still couldn't find her voice, though relief flooded her heart. Putting her foot all the way Antonio's behind would have felt nice, but would have consequences. After making sure that she was all right, he turned his attention back to Antonio.

"Weren't you already warned about messing with this beautiful woman?" he asked, barely holding on to his temper.

"She is *my wife*," Antonio said loudly before having the wind knocked out of him by one of the guards.

"Soon to be ex-wife," Hassan said through his teeth. "You can stew on that during your plane ride back home."

"I'm not going anywhere," Antonio protested. "I came here to see my mother. You can't make me leave,"

Hassan's normally clear laugh was tinged with sarcasm. "That's where you're wrong. You'll be on the first plane out of here. It's already been arranged. You should have made sure to see your mother, because you won't be able to do that now. It's time for you to go."

Antonio shot an angry look at Blair, then lunged forward.

Big mistake.

As she balled up her fist to land a low blow to his pride and joy, Hassan rushed forward, eyes blazing. He dragged Antonio away from her and punched him in rapid succession, almost lifting him off the floor with each blow.

She put her back to the wall, angered that this was all happening in the once place she could ill afford to make waves.

"You left the door wide open for someone else to recognize that she is a good woman," Hassan said, pushing him in the direction of the guards walking toward them. "Be mad, but don't be mad at her. Be mad at yourself. You screwed up."

Turning to Blair, he said, "Go home, jamila. I'll meet you there." Before she could protest about work, he explained, "Everything is taken care of and there is no more work today."

Blair moved towards the door, glancing over her shoulder in time to see Hassan smile. She smiled back, and Antonio's gaze narrowed on her. He should be grateful that Hassan came when he did. She would have put those three hard punches in a place where he'd still be wondering if he was a girl or boy.

She wound through the corridor on her way outside to Hassan's car. They needed to talk, and she needed time to process what happened with Antonio today.

* * *

Blair took in Hassan's solemn expression when he arrived, and realized that bad news was on the way. She wondered if something went wrong with him having Antonio transported back to the States. They had so much to talk about, and she wasn't sure where they should begin. He grabbed a bottle of Moscato and a wineglass before guiding her to their favorite place—the outside patio with that awesome view of the city skyline. The nighttime breeze provided a respite from the warmth that bathed Durabia earlier that day.

The fact that he poured her a full glass should have been a sign. The next words that he spoke were unexpected and heart wrenching.

"Until you are a free woman," he said in a low tone as he faced her on the sofa, "we need to limit how much time we spend together. And I can no longer remain in your home. I will be staying at a nearby until everything is sorted out."

She was right. Bad news. His was the first voice she heard in the morning and the last one at night. Every fear or doubt she had, he talked her through it. He was everything that a man should be to a woman. And just when she was starting to believe they had something real … this.

Pain slammed into Blair's heart when the true meaning of the separation hit. "Are you breaking up with …"

"No, Blair. First, this comes because I was reminded that I am a royal and my actions with you is totally against protocol. Second, I … I spoke with Dwayne, King of Lawndale, and he told me how American divorces can sometimes drag out for years and years if one of the parties continues to dispute. His wife's ex-husband did it out of spite. Your husband is equally vindictive."

"That won't happen with me," she protested.

"You didn't see the look in his eyes when I stepped off the plane in Chicago to greet you," Hassan said. "I should not have done that. Truly, I apologize, as it might have made things worse."

Blair absorbed his words. This man had become too much a part of her life, and it would be a little empty without him.

"The children really love you."

He put some distance between them, obviously resisting the urge to kiss her. "I love them too. The sunshine girl is so much like you—feisty."

Blair sighed and massaged her forehead. "What do I tell them?"

"The truth. That we love them and only want what's best for them."

"What do I tell my heart?"

"Same thing I'll tell myself every second of every day until I can be with you."

Blair thought of Lola, her sunshine girl and swallowed hard at the lump crowding her throat. The minute Hassan Ali Khan walked through the doors of their home, that curly-haired little minx was running to him with arms held up to greet him. He would scoop her up and twirl her around, bringing about giggles and laughter that echoed throughout the house.

Blair shook her head, backing herself away from the memory.

"It is going to be fine, Blair," Hassan said, breaking into her thoughts and placing his hand over hers. "It will just take time. I do not want this either, but my family …" He sighed. "Until you are able to truly commit to me, this is how things will be. I am of the age where my family is expecting me to be married and have my own family. I cannot be with a woman who continues to be tethered to someone else. My father has given me an ultimatum of sorts. Marry that foreign girl within a month or marry the girls he has arranged for me."

Although pain sliced her heart, Blair managed to say, "My fault. This is all my…I refused to let go, trying so damned hard to be right and … and…"

"Blair, don't."

She flinched and backed further away. "You were right. I was bitter and vengeful. I wanted to hurt him for every second of pain and embarrassment he caused me. I was so caught up in trying to make him pay, and now look at us. I'm stuck in a loveless marriage and you…" She raked a hand through her hair as she looked away. "You warned me, I didn't listen."

She looked back as Hassan sank down onto the sofa.

"Blair—"

"If nothing else, I can at least own my stuff," she whispered, before he could begin defending her as he always did. "You saw this coming, didn't you?"

Hassan nodded, a soft breeze lifting the corners of his dark, silky hair. "You had every right to be leery of me and life here at first, but yes. After a while it became tedious. I listened to you before you came, I built a whole world for you, a safe one where you didn't have to hurt anymore. Yet, still you held onto him, this marriage. And there I was, ready to apologize for something I didn't do… paying for something…" He looked up at her and winced at the pain he saw on her face.

Blair nodded as she ran a trembling hand over her mouth. "I never asked you to—"

"Of course not, but every day I had to deal with this emergency or that emergency, stemming from something you should have ended a year ago."

"But my children—"

"You knew what their father was," he countered. "You could have ended all of it before you came to the airport. You could have ended it after you settled in here. You know what I think? I think it was all about pride. You want to be right."

She bounded to her feet, almost knocking over the little glass table holding the remaining contents of the bottle. "That is not...."

Hassan sat back and crossed his legs, his eyes devoid of any judgement as he waited. When she didn't speak, he said, "Maybe just a little true. Why does everyone have to pay for your father leaving you?"

Her breath hitched as she tried to formulate the words, "I never..."

"Tell me I'm wrong," he said, putting his focus back on the skyline. "I'll believe you."

"I think you should go."

Hassan hesitated several moments, then stood and smoothed out his garment. "Maybe I should, because the woman I love isn't here. The woman I know is formidable at the hospital. That woman is ready to take on the world in *that* place. Imagine if she expended just a portion of that energy, that passion and love on herself. Then maybe she'd see how much I love her." Hassan moved to walk away then turned back to face her head on. "After a while, you'll get to a place where you're just done. You cut your losses, but you're done. You don't hang on. You don't stay broken. You make a choice and you stick by that choice." He placed his hand over hers. "Otherwise you're just lying to yourself and everyone around you who matters. I mean how can you possibly help someone else if you can't help yourself?"

Blair closed her eyes and grimaced as she took that in. "You make it sound so simple."

"There is nothing simple or easy about healing," he said, reclaiming the space beside her. "Trauma colors everything you do. No, it's not the least bit simple. It's a frightening thing, and it hurts, but you do it anyway. You have to or you just die alone, broken, and afraid. I can say it until the day I die, but it doesn't matter until you believe it." He gathered her hands in his. "Blair, you deserve better. I can see it. Your children—*our* children, know it. Why can't you?"

"You don't understand."

"I don't. You're right," he shot back. "I live with an overbearing father who wants to dictate my life but can't see that my mother is ill and she doesn't try for treatment because my father is insisting that nothing is wrong, and she doesn't defy him even though it's in her own best interest. I am bound by traditions thousands of years in the making with no account for who I am or what I want. I am a member of a family so wrought with betrayal and greed that they try to kill or ruin anyone in their path…" Hassan put his gaze squarely on her, an intensity in those dark brown depths. "I am envious because the children get to wake up to you, and every single night it gets harder and harder to say goodnight because I want to spend the night holding you, making love to you. I want to grow old with you and add to our family, but it's impossible to do that when you hold me at bay; when you have held onto to something that doesn't let you move on. Maybe you don't want me after all."

Blair parted her lips to speak but he held up a hand to halt whatever protest she was about to lodge.

"I've been standing in front of you with my arms open since you arrived. I've been fighting for you every single day. And for what? To watch you put yourself in harm's way for a man that would defile you in your marital bed because your names are both on a sheet of people." He inhaled and let it out slowly. "So here I stand doing the one thing I don't want to do, because I think enough of you to give you your space. And even if you don't want to grow old with me, here I am ready to walk away from my family." His gaze narrowed on her. "I've spent this last year fighting for you. Why won't you fight for me?" He shook his head. "You know what? Don't, I can follow doctrine and marry the women betrothed to me. I could even have children with them, but it would be half a life."

Blair stood stock still staring at Hassan. "One marriage is bad enough when it's a marriage of convenience or obligation. No, I wouldn't want that for you."

"I will give it all up," he whispered. "If you will allow me to call in some reinforcements and have this issue handled."

"Please just go," Blair said softly as her mood went further south. "You're willing to defy him about the marriage part, but not about the residence. We're not even having sex."

"It is an honorable thing that I do," he explained, his tone compassionate. "Giving you space to decide what you truly desire."

Blair tried to still the rapid beating of her heart that was splintering with every sign that she would lose him. "You've become such a part of my life, that … I just …" She sighed again, then straightened her shoulders. "I understand."

"I will take my leave." He gave her a slight bow. "My heart was set on… is still set on growing old with you. Funny how things work out."

Hassan trudged toward the glass doors, but glanced over his shoulder in time to see tears streaming down her face and heard the sob that escaped her lips. He rushed back to her and gathered her in his arms. "Please don't cry. The space you need, the time is only temporary, yes?"

"It's only been two minutes since you mentioned it and it already feels like forever," she whispered into his chest.

"I cannot get around family obligations," he said in a patient tone. "So many young Muslim men are already feeling the pinch behind Kamran's marriage to Ellena. My father, especially. Though we are far enough down the royal line that I will not be Sheikh, they are trying to make sure that I have no alternative but to do what they want. Marrying an expatriate has its own issues. Being with you the way I have since you arrived, is not without consequences."

Her jaw went slack as she looked up at him. "You can get in trouble?"

"Blair, I have been courting 'good' trouble from the moment I met you," he confessed, smiling. "Now it has caught up with me. If I marry you before that date, then—"

"You're off the hook?"

"There is a little less challenge on my end," he admitted. "I can handle that, but I cannot give this up for a one-sided love."

Blair pondered that for a while. "It's not fair that your father is playing games with your life. What about your uncle? He's the Sheikh. Can't he intervene?"

"That is something I will not ask him to do." He released her but kept his gaze fixed on her face. "This is my issue. I cannot go running to my uncle to fix my problems with the tribunal watching his every move."

Blair shook her head. "I'm not marrying a man who can have multiple wives," she admitted. "I just left a man who tried to be slick and pull that off by essentially making me and my best friend, sister wives. And to be honest, I miss my friend a hell of a lot more than I miss my husband." Blair bit down on her lip before she met his eyes. "But losing you would be ten times worse."

Hassan hauled her close and kissed her hard and deep.

"Good, because the only wife I need. The only wife I want is you."

"Then let's figure out a way to make that happen, Hassan."

Hassan kissed her hands and led her over to the sofa.

"Girdles and grey hair run in my family. You sure you want in on that?"

Hassan leaned in with a coconspirator's smile.

"I hear pot bellies and the occasional male pattern baldness run in mine."

Blair, and Hassan burst into laughter and embraced.

"But spending a lifetime with you would decorate my soul."

"Mine too. Where do we start?" Blair shrugged and basked in the light of his love and the promise of a newly forged common goal.

Chapter 19

There was a strange vibe in the operating room because it was Saturday, and also a Durabian holiday. Celebrations were underway all over the city. No one wanted to be at work with thoughts of the food, fun, festivities and free-flowing liquor happening while they were in this room with only the sound of 80's music playing and the hum of medical equipment to keep them company.

Blair had pulled an emergency colon case and grimaced when she saw the name of the surgeon. Dr. Ammar was one of Blair's least favorite to work with. He was proficient in his medical craft but always seemed unnecessarily anxious in dealing with his cases. The constant second-guessing and lack of confidence could eventually land him on the wrong side of a malpractice suit.

When he wasn't timidly working in the operating room, Dr. Ammar had a cocky aura. He believed he was better than most—even his fellow doctors. He had a tan complexion and a low-cut beard, green eyes flecked with gold, and eyebrows thick enough to take a nap in. He always talked about his red Mercedes Benz, how clean it was, and how fast it was to drive. He also mentioned that he managed to get out of a speeding ticket because he told the police he was a top surgeon. Blair couldn't fault him for that one. In Chicago, telling the police she worked in surgery was a line she had also used.

Blair always played music in the OR to set the mood before a procedure started. Sometimes the hum of the bear hugger—a machine to keep the patient's body warm while they sleep—could wear on a person's nerves. Not hers, though. The minute something "sounded" different Blair would know. Even with the music going, she monitored the normal echoes in the room which tipped her off quickly when something needed her attention. The other staff had that same skill set. The doctors, not so much. Rightfully so. Their focus was entirely different.

Dr. Ammar swept into the room, all five-feet-three inches of him. He smirked, and his first stop was to turn the music off. Everyone else in the room let out a collective groan. The incision start time was set at ten, and everything proceeded as normal. The lull of common sounds in the room tended to cause a hush of peacefulness to settle over everyone, which could be dangerous. Blair's relief nurse wasn't scheduled until three in the afternoon. Dr. Ammar was still working, but everyone was focused on closing.

The relief scrub nurse, Alia, finally showed her face and waited for Blair to do the instrument count. Alia was thin, a perfect likeness of Olive Oyl from one of Blair's childhood cartoons. The impatience and disdain rolled off her in waves. She believed that since she had been at Durabia Medical a year before the senior nurse on staff, she should be treated like a boss. Blair always thought everyone should act their "wage" and carry their own weight, but this one didn't get the memo.

Not to mention, Alia was really tight with the director and had managed to have several other nurses either transferred or even fired. She had her sights set on Blair from day one.

Blair always counted twice because once she had noticed they were off by four items, which meant an immediate X-ray to locate the missing equipment. This time, the count was *over* the amount of the original count. A rare occurrence—which normally meant the person who handled the count before Blair arrived had not noted it correctly. Blair kicked herself for not doing her own count because she did not want to offend her colleagues. She would not make that mistake again.

"We need to do an X-ray," Alia said, glaring at Blair and the circulating nurse. The staff performing the surgery could not move from the surgical field, or they could become contaminated.

Blair waited, remembering that she was still a relatively new scrub tech to this hospital and there was a lot she didn't know when it came to the way they handled procedures. Until something happened which necessitated questions. Like this one.

"Why do we have to do an X-ray on the patient since the count was over, not—"

"Because, if you were intelligent enough and had read the policies," Alia snarled through her teeth. "Then you would already know that—"

"Hold up," Blair snapped, and raised a gloved hand. "You mean if our clinical educator had given me that particular policy to read, then I would've known that without asking. I hear you. I'm right here in your face, so tone it down a notch. All I did was ask a question."

The vibe in the operating room grew tense.

"Throwing that little remark about what I should know was uncalled for. This hospital might do things a little different than Chicago. I need to know that, and I need to know why. If you're not up for answering in a respectful way, then I'll ask someone else."

Alia flinched, then growled, "You're new here, so I'll let that pass. But don't you dare address me in front of everyone like this."

"Like what?" Blair shot back. "In the same manner in which you addressed me? How unfair is that." Blair faced the doctor; whose focus was on the exchange and not on the patient as she winked at him. "You might want to close before she catches pneumonia."

He winked back, then put his attention on the procedure. So, did everyone else.

"We're both grown women. You're not going to talk to me any kind of way," Blair said to Alia. "I'll check you before you finish. Respect is earned, not given automatically." She inhaled and gave the woman a long look. "Now, let's try this again. Feel free to answer the question—respectfully or not at all."

The look in several pairs of wide eyes above the surgical masks was priceless. Even Dr. Ammar gave her a nod of respect.

Interesting. Maybe she could have a little talk with him about that music thing.

Hassan was right. Anything was possible. Now if only they could get a handle on arranging their marriage.

Chapter 20

"She needs a blood test," Hani, the consulate representative, said with a stern expression. "If she doesn't pass, the application will not move forward."

Blair shared a glance with Hassan. "Fine, I'll send over my results from the hospital."

"No, it must be done here." He leaned forward, resting his elbows on the wooden desk which held several personal photographs.

"Where does it say that?" Hassan moved forward, tapping an index finger on the edge of the document. "We read the fine print. Nowhere on the website or in the file you sent is that expressed."

"New policy," Hani answered with a shrug. "And yours is a ... *special* case. A royal marrying an expatriate."

"Expatriate?" Blair asked, frowning.

"People who reside in a country who weren't born there, or a natural citizen," Hani explained with a disdainful glare at Blair. "Unheard of in this part of the world."

"Until my uncle married Sheikha Ellena," Hassan corrected, and his tone was equally hard.

"Yes, there is that" Hani said in a sour tone that matched his expression. "The blood test needs to be done here in Durabia. By our physicians. We have her scheduled for next week."

"Is she able to do it tomorrow?" Hassan asked, glaring at the man who seemed a little nonchalant about this important matter.

"What's the rush?" Hani shrugged, a smug smile on his thin lips.

"We're sort of on a deadline here," Blair said, tightening her hold on Hassan's hand.

"Well, next week is the earliest you'll be seen. My apologies." He turned this back to them and reached into a cabinet drawer behind him.

As they left the office and made their way to the lobby, Blair asked, "Is it me or did he seem a little …"

"Insincere?" Hassan asked with both brows raised.

She tipped her head toward him. "I was going to say full of it, but that works, too."

"One week," Hassan said, placing a kiss on her temple. "Then we'll come back and have everything in order."

* * *

A week later, it took three attempts before they were able to get in front of Hani again. Almost as if he was dodging them on purpose.

"Ahhh, the love birds return," he said with a plastered-on smile. "Well, she passed. No diseases or anything that would—"

"You seem disappointed," Hassan snapped. He grabbed the chair and sat with an expression so thunderous Blair thought he was seconds away from snatching the man and giving him a good shake.

"Oh no, not at all," Hani replied smoothly, handing them the top page off a stack. "But now you'll need this signed by someone at the United States Embassy. You have an appointment with Mr. Fahim in a week."

"A week?"

Hani shrugged. "That is the earliest he can see you."

"I'll see what I can do," Hassan said to Blair.

This time Hani grinned as he handed Hassan a document. "He will tell you the same."

"A week? Really?" Hassan growled.

"Love is timeless," Hani quipped, grinning with a spiteful glint in his eyes.

"Yes, but deadlines are not," Hassan mumbled.

* * *

Blair left the embassy concerned by the feeling that everyone was working against them. Something was off. Way off, but she couldn't quite put her finger on it. She walked into work expecting to do the regularly scheduled surgeries for the day. All routine, nothing spectacular. Her first case was a Port-a-Cath Removal. Simple—the surgeon was scheduled to make a small incision and remove the catheter, which should have only taken about twenty minutes. Everyone else in the room was waiting for the patient to wake up so they could clear the area and prepare for the next surgery.

A distinct ringing cut through the normal background sounds of the room. Blair turned the music down, left the rolling chair and went to the far-right wall to pick up the phone.

"Hey Blair," Rashida, the Labor and Delivery nurse said on the other end. "Have you ever been in any L&D cases?"

Blair thought about it for a minute, then responded, "Once, I was pulled to help deliver a baby because they were short-staffed, but it's not my area of specialty."

"Well guess what," Rashida exclaimed. "We have an emergency C-section that's about to take place in twenty minutes. We need you to circulate for that case. The nurse that they have upstairs is not that experienced and she's going to need help in that room."

Blair inhaled and let it out slowly. A few years ago, when Blair was assigned to her first and only delivery, the parents gave Blair such a hard time she was ready to punch the nearest wall. When the mother was in labor, she complained to Blair about one thing but would tell the obstetrician a different story. That kind of behavior created confusion and could get the patient killed. After that, Blair decided to leave the hormones and chaos to someone else. This time, Blair was a little excited and nervous because of the emergency status. She glanced to her right and told Aniyah, "I need you to finish here."

"Where are you going," Aniyah asked, clearly uncomfortable with Blair being in the lead.

"Upstairs. Emergency C-Section."

"Why didn't they call for me?" Aniyah asked, scowling. "I usually do those."

Blair shrugged and was out the door, yanking the covering from around her neck, then tossing it into the hamper. She mulled over Aniyah's question. She did have a point. Why hadn't they called her? Blair was more suited to stay on the current case. Something must be really wrong for them to switch gears like that.

She took the elevator to the third floor, then made a left and walked to the nurse's station to meet with the charge nurse. The woman had a creamy complexion, brown eyes, and dark hair flowing down her back. She was good friends with the supervisor from Blair's department, so her relationship with Blair was tenuous at best. She handed over the report on Adara Muhammad.

"The patient didn't come in at the beginning of contractions. We found that she's been in labor for twenty hours," she said. "Her pressure is rising, and the baby is in a breech position."

Blair rushed alongside Parvez, the spiky-haired anesthesiologist, as they brought the patient directly to the OR. Once the patient was situated in the center on the OR bed and strapped securely, Blair cleared her throat. "Anesthesia, time out please."

The time out process was a universal protocol that made sure of the patient's identity, and that the right procedure was being performed at the correct surgical site. During a time out, everyone paused and listened to the circulating nurse speak.

"We have patient Adara Muhammad in the room," Blair said, scanning the documentation. "No allergies, and two grams of Ancef has been given." The medication was an antibiotic used to treat a wide variety of bacterial infections. There had been cases where a patient made it through surgery just fine, but infection could make recovery time longer and more difficult.

Blair put a "smile" in her voice as she asked, "Ms. Muhammad, can you please state your first and last name and date of birth please?"

The patient, looking nervous as most patients tended to do when they were about to put their lives in someone else's hand, complied with the command.

Parvez began the process of putting the patient to sleep, and Blair and her team performed a series of scrubs, cleaning the belly and getting the patient ready for the surgeon. Blair switched the music to Reggae and her co-workers started to get a little groove going.

Dr. Akbar entered the room with a solemn, "Good afternoon, everyone."

"Good Morning," everyone responded, standing at their various stations, and waiting for his next commands.

Dr. Akbar had scrubbed in, then the surgical tech gowned and gloved him before assisting with draping the patient and creating the rest of the sterile field.

"Time out, please," Blair said again to begin the second check. "We have patient Adara Muhammad, birthday, four, twenty-six, nineteen eighty-three. We are here to perform a Cesarean section and the consent form has been signed. No known allergies are listed, and Sequential Compression Devices are in place." The SCD's were vital because they prevented excess blood flow in the legs during and post-surgery.

"Does everyone agree?"

They did and the procedure began.

"Incision time, 12:09," Blair stated.

Nearly forty minutes later, the doctor said, "At 12:45 p.m., an eight-pound-nine-ounce baby girl was born." Blair took the baby from the surgeon and immediately gave the infant to the L&D nurses who were on standby. Ms. Muhammad was semi-conscious as the L & D nurses wheeled her out of the room and off to recovery. The nurse put a suction bulb in the baby's mouth to get the fluid out, and her cries echoed in the room.

Joy filled Blair's heart, but it was short-lived as one of the L&D nurses said, "There's something awkward about the baby's genitals."

Blair walked across the room, craned her neck, and found that the baby did seem to have an abnormal vagina. A nodule protruded from the base of the skin of the labia.

The surgeon walked over to the baby to do an examination of his own. "It seems as though this baby has a sexual development disorder."

Blair had already determined that the baby was born as what they termed "intersex". While most humans were born with either a vagina or penis, at times there are others born with both genitals, or sometimes with testicles that are malformed or absent.

Decades ago, doctors in America would perform the cosmetic surgery unbeknownst to the parents. Most didn't realize a decision had been made until the child reached puberty. Then, the female would develop decidedly masculine features such as a beard and hairy chest or the male would suddenly grow breasts. Not to mention, their voices would lean toward the opposite of the "sex" they presented.

Dr. Akbar locked gazes with the anesthesiologist and said, "I can fix this problem." Then told the team, "I need new surgical instruments. I'm going to scrub in again."

Alarmed, Blair left her spot near where the baby was situated to face him. "We're doing a procedure on the baby right now?"

"We're going to perform an IGM," the surgeon answered.

"An Intersex Genital Mutilation? Now?" she shot back. "Oh so, there's another consent signed by the parent, right?"

Dr. Akbar froze, then glared at her.

"Did you get consent from the mother?" she pressed as everyone waited. "Because the last time I laid eyes on her, she was still semi-unconscious and wasn't able to make heads or tails of anything."

"I don't need consent for this procedure," Dr Akbar snapped. His terse response changed the atmosphere in the room.

"You need a consent for any and every surgery procedure, Dr Akbar," Blair said, and all the staff looked her way. "It's a universal protocol."

"This is *my* operating room," he said between his teeth. "And I'm making the call on this. Feel free to leave."

Blair hesitated, trying to figure out the best course of action while the team members trudged to the various stations, preparing for the procedure. The doctor was well aware that Blair couldn't leave the room until both patients were clear. Abandoning a patient could cause her to lose her license. She'd never had to deal with this situation before.

Instead, she went to a tablet and typed an incident report on the case.

If there were going to be any legal issues, she wanted her objection documented. Blair ensured that she emailed a copy to herself and also took a screenshot.

"What are you doing?" Dr. Akbar demanded, causing everyone to look in her direction.

"Covering my ass. When what you did comes to light, it'll leave the hospital, you, me, and everyone here open for a lawsuit. I'm simply making sure that my protest over this procedure and your refusal to obtain the proper consent is well-documented. All because you're trying to play God with this child and taking the decision from the parents. If anyone's going down for this, it's not going to be me."

Blair had read about people struggling from intersex issues. Children who didn't find out all the details of their birth until they were teenagers. It wasn't fair to make a decision for a person who couldn't make it for themselves. These surgeries could cause long-term issues with sexual function and sensation if not handled correctly.

If the parents made the decision, they had the right to deal with it the best way they saw fit and tell the child when they felt it necessary. To be honest, Blair didn't feel the parents should alter their child until the child was able to make a decision. But to have someone else make that decision for them without their knowledge, leaving the child and family to be confused and scared when abnormal symptoms showed up later, was not only unethical, but would leave this hospital open for a world of costly lawsuits and take everyone in this room along for the ride.

Dr. Akbar placed the knife on the tray and said, "We'll wait until the parents sign the consent."

"Yes," Blair said with a smile. "That sounds about right."

His glare let her know this would not be the end of the story. And with Salimah gunning for Blair's job since day one, insubordination would be all the ammunition she needed.

Chapter 21

Hassan walked into the consulate, barely keeping it together. The office they were directed to had an Ekintop desk with a six-foot brown shelf full of books. Comfortable leather furniture was arranged on the right side of the room for clients to sit close to tall, glass windows. Hassan struggled to keep his temper in check.

"You did not bring the signed copy from the U.S. Embassy?" hani asked Blair.

"They told us we only needed *these* documents," she said, placing the package in front of him.

"Oh yes, but he needs permission to sign this and marry an expatriate," Hani said with a lack of patience, then pushed the documents back to them. "Sorry, but there is nothing I can do. This is a special case."

"If we get this one signed today, can we come back here?"

"Of course." Hani turned his attention to the screen, ready to blow them off. "In a week's time."

"Wait a minute," Blair protested. "We've already been here twice."

"Yes, without the proper documentation," he said in a droll tone, still not bothering to look at the forms. "That is not my problem. See you in a week."

They remained in their seats, dumbfounded at the level of incompetence between the two agencies.

Finally realizing they were still there, he asked, "Is there something else I can help you with?"

"No, you've done quite enough," Hassan said, getting to his feet, extending a hand to Blair.

Blair could tell he was trying to maintain a bland expression as they cleared the threshold.

"Are you thinking what I'm thinking?"

"Yes. As my grandmother once said," Blair answered, "Something in the milk ain't clean."

"There is that." He pulled Blair into his arms. "I'm going to call the Embassy first and make sure we have everything in order."

"Sounds good."

* * *

"Ah, marriage. Love," Hani sighed, clasping his hands as though ready to dive into a meal. "A many splendored thing." He frowned as he scanned the application and documents. "Where is the paperwork from the Office of the Secretary of State?"

Hassan gripped the edge of the chair. "You did not mention that over the phone or when we were last here."

"Because I thought you had it already," he said with a shrug. "I can't do anything without *that* particular document."

Hani reached over and grabbed the phone. "Here, I'll contact him and see if he can scan it and send it over." He made the call, grimaced and his shoulders drooped dramatically.

When he turned, Blair held up one hand. "Don't tell me, he won't have it until next week."

Hani looked at the phone that was still in his hand, then to her, asking, "You heard that?"

"No, but it seems that everyone is singing that same song," Blair said, narrowing a gaze on him.

Hassan placed a hand on her thigh, a move that didn't go unnoticed by Hani. "We are becoming a little upset about the games you all are playing."

Hani feigned an innocent expression. "I have the request right here. See?" He placed the documents in front of them and tapped the edge of the desk. "No games. Now you just run along to the United States Embassy and everything will be fine."

"Is there anything else we need before they ping-pong us back here," Blair asked, standing along with Hassan.

"No," Hani's smile had an edge that betrayed his mild tone of voice. "Not that I can think of. Have a great day."

Blair and Hassan swept from the room. With a terse note in his voice, Hassan said, "That was easy."

"Too easy."

Chapter 22

"She will need permission from a father," Fahim pushed a new document their way across his glossy desk. The US Embassy seal glinted on the wall behind him. His eyes were steady, but Blair was sure she caught a hint of spite. Her jaw dropped and she all but sputtered. "I—I … I haven't spoken to Eric Senior in years. I don't even know where he is …"

"Well, there you have it," Fahim tossed their application aside. "No marriage."

Hassan's hard glare landed on her. "You do not know where—"

"Hassan," Blair said in a warning tone.

Duly chastised of his own lack of patience and understanding, he exhaled. "My apologies, my love. Maybe your mother can assist?"

"She hasn't heard from him, either."

Hassan absorbed that sad fact as his gaze skimmed the tidy desk, bland beige wall, and matching blinds. "Give me whatever information you have. We will hire someone to locate him."

"We are almost out of time," she protested. "What if they don't find him?"

"Go to work and do not worry." He handed her his car keys and texted his brother to pick up one of Hassan's other cars to come and pick him up.

Blair turned from him, her shoulders lowered in defeat. He waited until she was out of earshot before whirling to face Fahim. "My father has a hand in this?"

"I do not know what you mean," he answered, but wouldn't look Hassan in the eye.

"This … game you are playing with my life," he growled. "It will not be forgotten."

"It is not my fault you are marrying a girl from ..." He crooked his fingers as quotes, taunting, "Da hood. Good luck with that. Do not get angry with us because you are choosing to marry beneath you."

"Watch how you speak of her," Hassan warned. "She is my beloved and an American just like you."

Undeterred by the threat, Fahim shrugged. "She is low class and undeserving of being a royal."

"How long have you worked here?"

Fahim frowned, his olive complexion sallow under the artificial light. "A few years."

"And you bear such hatred and prejudice in your heart for a fellow countrywoman?"

Fahim's face turned a bright red. "There are plenty of white women and Durabians to choose from, yet you scrape from the bottom. I don't see why you could not just sleep with her and be done. Satisfy your curiosity and lust and do as your family expects."

"My family?'

Fahim blanched. "If you're so keen on marrying outside of your status, I have a daughter who—"

"Probably is as racist, bigoted, and misguided as you are," Hassan fired back. "I have no desire to be attached to someone who has the audacity to insult not only an entire group of people, but the Sheikha as well."

For a moment, Fahim shrank back. He was half Arabic and half White. "This is the United States Embassy," he said, his arrogance returning. "Durabian royalty has limited authority here."

"True, but we can request that the person who represents America on Durabian soil does not have a racist or bigoted heart. How can you serve all Americans if you do not like half of them?"

Fahim's face fell into an irritated scowl and he squared his shoulders. "Good day to you."

Hassan stormed from the office but made a mental note to have a conversation with his uncle regarding the exchange. American prejudice might run rampant on U.S. soil, but it would not be tolerated in Durabia. Sheikh Kamran was making sure of this.

He swept out of the building and walked across the street, still incensed about the exchange. He texted Daron Kincaid about locating Blair's stepfather, the man who had a hand in raising her.

A strawberry blonde with a pretty, angular face ran up to him and tapped his arm. "Excuse me, Mr. Khan."

Hassan stopped and faced her. "Yes?"

"I work inside the embassy." She glanced over her shoulder and stared back at him; her eyes filled with anxiety. "If you don't mind, I'd like to tell you something."

"Sure." He directed her to move away from the sight of the front entrance.

She kept her tone just above a whisper. "It might cost my job."

"Then you should consider whether you should be forthcoming," he said, understanding her expectation without being told in so many words. "I cannot promise to save or replace your position. I have no authority in that regard."

She grimaced, disappointment in her expression. "I understand."

"But thank you all the same."

"My pleasure."

He barely heard her response above the sound of traffic as he turned to where his brother, Akeem, awaited.

"Sir ..."

Hassan realized she was struggling with whether to give him the information she had or walk away.

"What he's not telling you is that the permission needs to be from her *biological* father, not her stepfather. He is not being honest. He said 'a' father on purpose to mislead you. Your father does not wish for this marriage to happen. All of them are working together to frustrate you." She placed a hand on his arm, thought better of it, and let it fall to her side. "If he's alive, he needs to be here, or they will nullify the marriage even if you go through with it. You won't know it until it's too late. That's what they're counting on."

Hassan tamped down on his anger. "Thank you so very much. Please keep this card," he said, laying a hand on her shoulder. "If anything negative transpires because of your willingness to help me, please contact me. I cannot promise that I can safeguard your employment here, but I will make sure you are all right."

"Thank you." She lowered her gaze to the pavement. "That might happen sooner than you think. There are cameras everywhere."

His gaze went to his brother, who waited patiently, then said, "Why would you risk—"

"Because it's wrong," she replied, shaking her head. "And I'm a hopeless romantic."

He smiled. Truthfully, he was too. He just hadn't realized until Blair came along.

"Thank you."

Hassan watched her walk away, then made it to the car and was on the phone to Daron within seconds. "Change of plans. We need to locate Blair's *biological* father instead. And let us figure out what we need to carry out an American wedding. Things are too hot in Durabia right now."

Daron was silent a moment then said, "I wouldn't mention that aspect to Blair right now."

"Blair needs to know." Hassan fixed his tie as he looked out the window.

"Whoa, wait a minute. Why?"

"Secrets and lies have cost my beloved more than you can possibly imagine. I cannot be a party to something, no matter how well intentioned, that will bring her more pain." Hassan moved to turn the key in the ignition, thought better of it and sat back.

"At least give us a chance to search for him before you say anything."

Hassan tapped the sun visor and it lowered. A picture of Blair stared back at him. The idea of getting her hopes up and dashing them made him sick inside. He took in a shaky breath.

"Do all that you can. If it goes south. If you can't find him, it's on me."

"We're on it," Daron said.

When he disconnected the call, Akeem looked across at him from the passenger. "That will not absolve you of your requirement to marry the women father has chosen for you. A marriage in America does not supersede a Durabian one." His thick brows drew together as he continued, "If you don't complete the requirements on this end, you're screwed. Blair will not be happy with being a third wife and doing things this way means that she will not be considered first wife. That is important. In order for you to have the marriage that will make Blair

Swanson happy, she needs to be *first* wife."

Yes, he was well aware of that fact. That is what made their situation all the more challenging.

* * *

"What are you making," Fatimah asked Brandon and Bella, who were seated at the play table in the parlor.

"It's an origami crane," Brandon answered, keeping his focus on the papers in his hands.

"It is beautiful," she said, picking up one of the tiny paper creations. "Will you show me how to do one?"

He bobbed his head and gave her a brilliant smile. "Sure."

"What is it for?" She examined the crane with narrowed eyes.

Brandon glanced at Bella, who shook her head and pulled away. "We can't tell you."

"Why?" Fatimah's voice held a tinge of alarm.

"We just can't," Bella said, shrugging.

Fatimah peered at them a moment, then back at the work they were doing. "Is it something ... evil?"

"No, ma'am," Brandon and Bella said unison.

"Then explain to me what it is for," she demanded, allowing the paper to fall from her hands.

"We can't tell you," Bella said, sliding a wary glance at her brother.

Fatimah's eyes widened with horror. "You must—"

"Come with me." Blair pulled Hassan's mother aside, guiding her to the kitchen. "Believe them when they say they can't tell you. They did one of these when my mother-in-law was going in for surgery. It is a wish for someone to get well."

"But Olivia's fine now," Fatimah protested. "We speak every day. And we take the children to the museum and other places."

"Yes, *she* is fine," Blair answered. "But she's not the only one in their lives who is not well. And they cannot tell the person it's intended to help."

"But who—" Her dark-brown eyes widened with understanding. "Oh, my word. Are they fashioning these cranes for…?"

"Yes, ma'am. Senbazuru is an ancient belief that when one folds one thousand origami cranes, their wish would come true. The process is also a symbol of hope and healing during challenging times."

Fatima blinked at the tears welling her eyes.

"So, you see, if *they* tell you, their wish won't come true." Blair placed her hand over Fatimah's on the counter. "And they want that for you because they love you. I'd like for you to come with me to see Jaidev and let him start the process of finding out why you are having stiffness and tremors in your hands."

"Do you truly think he can?" Her eyes held a touch of doubt but also hope.

"I do. We need you here." Blair, who had been paying close attention, suspected Fatimah was suffering from slow progressing Parkinson's Disease but was certain Jai could make a diagnosis and even administer some type of treatment, holistic and otherwise. Hassan had mentioned that his father had forbidden his mother to seek treatment of any kind. That an "illness" was all in her head.

"Fatimah, I want you here so that you're able to enjoy your life, travel with us, be there for the children your sons will have. I know that Yousef has a different take on things, but you have to look out for your own health. You deal with everything, not your husband. You."

"All right, I will do as you ask," she whispered.

"See?" Blair said with a smile as they sat opposite each other at the table. "Their wish is on its way to becoming true."

Fatimah sighed and looked down at her fingers. "Ellena was the very first Black woman I ever met. We are kept behind the palace walls, and the only people we interact with are family, and visiting dignitaries. I loved how Sheikha Ellena stood up to Sheikh Kamran's father."

"Yes, my aunt can be a little bold."

"And she's not the only one." Fatimah propped her chin on one hand. "When my son talks about you, I hear the happiness in his voice. I noticed it even before you arrived." She waved her hand in a dismissive way. "My husband means no harm; it is just that he is mired in the old ways. Our marriage was arranged. I have come to honor and respect him. But love? That is a different matter. He is a hard man to love and I realize now that is so important. I want my sons to have happy marriages. Hassan is embracing Sheikh Kamran's desire to change the way Durabia works." Fatimah lowered her gaze to the tabletop. "When he worked with the contractors to complete this place, he … how do you say it … cracked the whip, because he wanted this to be perfect. Even in the car he bought for you that you know nothing about."

Blair flinched and narrowed a gaz on her. "Wait, what?"

"In the garage. That Lexus is yours."

"Why wouldn't he—"

A sweet smile spread across Fatimah's face. "Because he loves taking you everywhere, and it gives him an excuse to spend time with you in public."

Blair laughed as delight and love for Hassan squeezed her heart. "All right. I won't tell him that I know if you won't."

Fatimah chuckled, and her smile was so much like Hassan's Blair had to catch her breath.

"You are a smart woman. Do not let the machinations of my husband or your unhappy past deter you from your path," Fatimah said, "Hassan is coming for dinner at eight. Get dressed, I will tell you his favorite place. You two go out and have some fun."

Chapter 23

"Well, it's not like we haven't done it before," Daron Kincaid said, settling on the couch between Shaz and Jai, across from Dro, Dwayne and Vikkas. Blair had prepared an array of food and beverages for their guests—six members of the Kings of the Castle. The spread provided an eyeful on the heavy oval table that was pressed into service for this gathering.

Shaz adjusted his locs so they flowed down his back. "What?"

"Shotgun weddings," Dro supplied, crossing one slack-covered leg over the other.

"When did that ever happen?" Shaz frowned.

"Temple and Jai."

"That wasn't a shotgun wedding," Jai protested, taking a sip of moscato.

"We were still under the gun," Dro admitted with a slow nod. "I can't believe that we pulled it off."

"At least their family drama wasn't anything like Milan's," Daron teased, fingering the edge of his fedora as he contemplated the incident with Vikkas' blood relatives.

"Oh man, that had me reeling," Shaz said, laughing. "First time I ever saw Khalil mad enough to shoot someone."

"And Jai's housekeeper gave him the means to do it," Vikkas said, shifting his gaze to his brother, Jai. "Who names their gun Roscoe?"

"Evidently, a woman who knows how to use it." Jai lifted his glass in mock salute, the others did the same.

"All right, what do you need us to do?" Daron asked, cutting through the chatter.

"My father had given me four weeks to marry Blair or I'll have to marry the two women he's arranged for me. I'm now down to a few days. I just found out from my mother that he's actually been giving Blair's ex money to drag out the divorce past my deadline, even going so far as to fly him over here to cause trouble. So now I'm down to drastic measures."

Shaz looked to Daron and asked, "So, what are the most important steps we need to take?"

Hassan laid a hand on Blair's wrist. "Would you mind bringing me a cold glass of sparkling grape juice?"

She narrowed her gaze on him and quirked an eyebrow. "If you need to speak with them without me being around, just say so."

A tiny smile curved his lips. "Blair, I would like to speak with your uncles in private."

She gave him the evil eye before sweeping out of the room. At the threshold, she said over her shoulder. "So, you don't actually need that drink, right?"

"Well, if it is not too much trouble, my love."

Blair paused and said, "You'd better be glad you added that last part."

The Kings chuckled as she sauntered away.

"I need Blair's divorce papers signed and her *biological* father's approval," Hassan said, letting his gaze settle on each man for a moment. "And I would prefer that we do not mention that part to her until we secure his help." He looked slowly around the group of men. "I would also like the paperwork put on a faster track because the embassy has been giving us all kinds of issues. They have been bouncing us back and forth between the U.S. Embassy and the Durabian Embassy, giving us half-truths and misinformation each time, since ours is a special case that doesn't follow traditional process." He sat forward on the seat. "I'm a royal marrying a nonbeliever, and expatriate. They are telling me that a host of problems come with that, even though I know they are not being quite right about things. Blair should still be considered a royal by her aunt's marriage to my uncle. But they are saying she only has that status when a marriage to me takes place and any offspring come as a result of the marriage."

"Why can't we get Sheikh Kamran involved," Shaz asked, putting a glance on Hassan. "That would immediate put an end to all of this."

Hassan shook his head. "He is already fighting his own battles when it comes to interfaith and interracial marriages. The tribunal has his feet to the fire. If he sided with us on this one, it would not bode well with him while he is fleshing out the details of how these types of issues will work."

"No worries, we'll do what needs to be done," Dro said.

Hassan sighed and let out his breath slowly. "Thank you, but I must tell you there might be one small problem."

Daron's eyebrows shot up as he waited for Hassan to speak.

"Blair hasn't laid eyes on her biological father in twenty years."

"So, Daron, I mean you're the tech guru and all," Jai hedged. "With your tech skills we can get around—"

"No, my brother," Daron answered with a shake of his head. "Not for this one. We have to do things in Durabia above board. Even with Temple and Jai in Chicago, no matter what I could manage on my end, they still had to put physical face time at City Hall to get that certificate. I don't want anything or anyone to unravel their union after the fact. And we could've gone through the back door, but their marriage was too important to take a chance by doing some behind the scenes tech manipulation. Same here." He tapped a point on his screen. "And the difference is, Durabia has a small circle of people who are connected to each other. All it will take is one phone call to verify that someone didn't dot an I or cross some T's for the marriage to be null and void." He pulled out his tablet and began rapidly typing. "In Chicago, no one would bat an eye. But here, Hassan must keep his boots on the ground, moving that paperwork through, playing whatever Three-card Monte they've got going on."

Dro clasped a hand on Daron's shoulder. "We, on the other hand, have to locate Blair's father, have a conversation with her ex, and maybe a talk with the judge."

Dwayne perked up. "Who's handling the divorce?"

"Judge Breedlaw."

"A familiar name," Dwayne said of the judge who was instrumental in keeping Dwayne's beloved from being embroiled in a six-year ordeal with an ex who just wouldn't let go.

"And you'll need this," Blair said, entering the discussion as she walked back into the room. "I fired my attorney because he seemed to be working against me. So, here's a screenshot of the document my ex made me sign before he let me take the children out of America."

"This is good." Daron scanned the text in the photo. "Let's make moves."

Chapter 24

"Why won't you help us?"

Blair had already purchased non-refundable tickets to visit Chicago and scheduled everything down to the letter to get Antonio's signature on those papers. When she received the phone message from one of her younger cousins back in the states.

"We're gonna end up just like Calla," the girl whined before the line went dead.

Blair remembered her cousin peering at her from the upstairs window in Grandma Ruth's house. The few times Blair asked to see and play with her older cousin, the idea was nixed and Blair was redirected to some other activity. That is, until she heard the screams. By the time it was over, the house was swarming with police and other strangers. Calla's body was being escorted out of the house in a black bag and Grandma Ruth was carrying a small warm bundle to the ambulance.

The stories became whispers, and the premature child never made it past the first year. Unfortunately, the bloodstain was still there, and no one was allowed on the third floor of Grandma Ruth's house.

The Kings were talking about squaring things in five days. That was cutting it too close as she didn't have that kind of time. She planned to make it to the States tonight in just enough time to get those papers signed, even if she had to shoot Antonio to get it done.

She had one last matter to handle before she made it to the airport. She arrived to work and was told by Salimah, the director of nursing, "Well, since Zaina hasn't been trained to take on the cases slated for you, you'll need to stay because no one can properly handle things in your absence."

Stunned, Blair just glared at her and said, "I emailed Zaina several times to meet with me. She blew me off. I even offered to have lunch several days in a row. She didn't bother to respond. I've been ready and willing, but she's not able, and that is not on me." Looking at her boss with a stern expression, Blair continued, "The only way I'm giving up my trip to Chicago is if you personally call and explain to the Chicago judge why I have to miss an emergency court hearing. And if you reimburse me for my plane tickets." Blair snatched a pen from her tote bag and scribbled something on the notepad on the desk. "Here's the number. I'll wait."

Salimah glared at her so long, Blair thought her eyes would become stuck that way. "You'll be written up for this. Next time, don't schedule anything until after you're sure your replacement is up to speed."

"And since this came at the last minute, and Zaina didn't make herself available, how was I supposed to do that?" Blair crossed both arms over her chest. "I would love your insight on that."

Silence.

"You've been hard on me since the first day I arrived," Blair said.

"I'm not sure what to do about that either, but I can speak to the director and see about being transferred to a different rotation. Maybe then you won't be so unfair about applying these arbitrary directives."

Salimah shuffled the papers in front of her. "I don't know what you're talking about."

"Let me give you my thoughts," Blair said, shifting in the seat to get comfortable. "For an employee to be indispensable is quite rare these days. I don't have some Black Girl Magic skills that you all depend on, where no one else can cover my shift or cases. It shouldn't be difficult for Aniyah or Oma to fill in because they definitely have the skill set. They've been working with me, learning from me, just like I'm learning from them. Zaina doesn't do that. She tries hard not to take *any* cases that will mean staying over her shift. She also manages to land the surprisingly easy cases, while leaving the hardest ones for the rest of us."

Blair gathered her things. "So, if you're threatening to fire me, then that means it's because you want to, not because you need to. That's a whole different beast right there. Because it also means you don't want to be bothered to do what it takes to actually make Zaina earn her keep like the rest of us."

She stood and met Salimah's heated gaze. "You may not care about keeping good employees, but those up the food chain do. Hiring and training new employees is not an inexpensive process. So, let me know how you want this to go. I leave for a preplanned and properly documented trip to handle some personal business and you fire me because my co-worker couldn't make time to do a few rotations with me, or we let this ride. Let me know what you decide and I'll gather up my documentation so I can handle everything when I return."

* * *

"What do you mean she's gone?" Hassan snapped, his anger threatening to get the best of him. He, along with the Kings, were supposed to be wheels up in three days as the private detectives were honing in on what they needed. His men were supposed to keep tabs on Blair so that no harm befell her in Durabia. As if it could. Durabia had the lowest crime rate of all the countries of the world, but knowing the lengths that the old guard would go since they were royals who were high ranking members of The Durabian Tribunal—he wasn't taking any chances.

"I dropped her off at the airport a few minutes ago," said Raheim, the bodyguard, who had been Blair's escort. "She's boarding a flight home."

"This is her home," Hassan growled, pounding his fist on the chest of drawers. The fact that she could be on the way home to confront her husband alone was alarming. The man practically assaulted her the last time she was in Chicago. "Is one of the private planes on the ground?"

"Yes, but she took a commercial flight."

"I'm commandeering uncle's private plane. I want to be in the air in the next thirty minutes." Hassan said, grabbing a small travelling case.

"Yes sir," Raheim said, pulling out his cell. "What is going on?"

Hassan yanked a few outfits out of his hotel closet and threw them in the suitcase. "She's trying to get to her husband to finalize the divorce."

"That is a good thing, no?"

"Not if she's going to see him alone," he said. "Did she receive any calls?"

"One, but I don't think it was from a man. Her voice was softer like she was trying to soothe a child."

"Then she also had darker business. She's headed into the mouth of the beast uncovered. This cannot happen. Not on my watch. I don't trust him…any of them. Call Dro Reyes. It is time we allow Ellena's brothers to have a face to face with that man sooner than they thought."

* * *

"Blair Swanson is on her way to America to finalize the divorce," Hani said to Yousef. "Once those papers are in place, we will not be able to stall any longer. They were already suspicious of my actions."

Yousef stared across his office space and sighed, thinking of the next steps. "Do you have a connection at the United States Embassy?"

"Yes, I do."

"Give them a call," he demanded, standing from behind his desk. "I would like to speak with them personally this time."

Hani retrieved his cellphone. "What are you going to do?"

"Buy us some more time. Throw some more money at her scum of a husband. No divorce means no marriage to Blair Swanson, and then my son must do as I command."

* * *

"Just sign the damn papers already," Blair demanded, thrusting the papers toward Antonio. "You can have the house, the car, even the child support you refuse to pay, just sign them. I'm not asking for anything from you. You can keep it. All if it."

He sprawled on their living room couch acting as if he didn't have a care in the world.

"You got what you wanted. Now let me live my life."

Antonio shrugged and propped his feet on the coffee table. "You can have a life."

"Not if I'm still tied to you."

"Is that such a bad thing?" he taunted. "We still have children. So, we're always going to be tied."

"Not like this." She held up one hand. "Sign the papers."

"You waited all this time. Why the sudden change? I figured you were playing mind games trying to see if we could still make it."

Blair reached into her waistband, then raised the gun.

"How's this for a mind game?"

"Wait," he yelled, his eyes widening with shock. "Is that a gun? What do you need that for?"

"Given how stupid you were last time..." She smirked and steadied her hand.

"You're still my wife!" He leaned back.

"That bullshit is not going to fly. Sign these and be done."

Hassan was right. She'd been sleep-walking through this whole thing; afraid to have her children raised in a single parent household, unwilling to let Antonio off the hook for what he owed them. How had she let it go this long?

"How much is it worth to you?" Antonio taunted, pulling her out of her thoughts.

"What?"

"Don't play dumb," he snapped. "You heard me."

"You already have money." Blair bumped the table Antonio had his feet propped up on causing them to slide to the floor. "More than I ever made."

"Yeah, but not more than *he* does." He leaned forward resting his elbows on his thighs, smirking. "I want some of that oil money. You know, to grease my palm and all that."

Unfreakingbelievable. "You're punishing me. You slept with Netty and I had enough presence of mind to know that's not the kind of married life I want." Looking down at him with a little sadness in her heart. "Truthfully, at first I missed her more than I missed you. But now? You two deserve each other."

"You were never there for me," he muttered. "Always kept me at a distance. And she was something to do." Antonio waved off the thought. "She was after me from day one. I just availed myself of what she had to offer. She was all tits and ass, but you had the brains. You were going somewhere, and I had every intention of going along for the ride. No big deal. You were working all the time, so she practically did you a favor."

"Seriously?" Blair nearly choked on that one word. "Is there a name for what's wrong with you?" Blair planted one fist on her hip and kept the gun pointed at him. "See, you talk fast and think I'm listening slow, but that's not the case. Sign the damn papers."

A knock on the door snatched her attention. When she backed up to it, opened it, and peered outside, three familiar men stepped forward. They walked into the house as if they owned it.

Antonio almost pushed her out of the way. "And who the hell are you?"

"Daron Kincaid," said one of them as he took the fedora off his head.

The handsome, dark-haired man next to him said, "Dro Reyes" as he took the gun from Blair's hand.

Then Hassan Ali Khan stepped over the threshold and said, "We need to have a little chat."

"Oh, so it's like that now?" Antonio taunted, giving Hassan a disdainful onceover. "This raghead's got you covered?"

Dro, Hassan, and Daron were in Antonio's space in the time it took to blink.

"I am a lot of things," Hassan said through his teeth. "That is not one of them. I am not the one who mistreated my wife, slept with her best friend, then left my wife to pick up the slack because the only thing I was paying was lip service." Hassan lifted one of his eyebrows as he glared at Antonio. "So, tell me, who is the real raghead around here."

Dro grimaced and both he and Daron moved forward to block Hassan's path to Antonio.

"And I'm not talking about color or ethnic background either," Hassan moved closer to Antonio's face. "I'm talking about your actions. I would actually call you the P-word, but that would be an insult to women everywhere." Hassan's voice rose as he said, "Sign the damn papers."

Chapter 25

When Aunt Dorsey learned Blair was back home in Chicago, she asked her to come over and talk. Blair had already made plans to visit while searching for her father, so maybe this was a good time. Blair was hoping not to walk into drama, but that couldn't be avoided since Dorsey had planned a family dinner including Christian, the children, and her sisters.

"Why didn't you come to me instead of calling DCFS?" Dorsey screamed. "You knew I would want to handle something like this myself. You're just selfish, stirring up drama as always."

"Oh, I'm sorry." Blair put a hand dramatically on her chest, her voice echoing the length of Dorsey's house. "Was I supposed to forget that you single-handedly destroyed my farewell dinner by inviting Grandma? Or was I supposed to conveniently forget that you're the reason I've missed ten years of Thanksgiving dinners, since you insist that your pervy husband be there. Despite the fact that your granddaughters both told you that he did something to them? Granddaughters you're raising because your daughters are strung out on drugs, trying to mask the pain of what you allowed to happen."

"They misinterpreted what he did," she said, waving away that thought with a dismissive hand.

"Did Calla misinterpret things too as she bled to death on the floor of her bedroom giving birth to her brother?" she said, and her heart hurt all over again. "And what about Tiffany? Did she somehow catapult herself onto the bed while they were roughhousing pantless? Did she want him to do the things he did to her," Blair snapped. "It was just a lucky accident that dislocated her shoulder, right? Get the hell out of here."

"You had no right to involve the government in my life." Dorsey shook a fist in her face. "We could've kept it within the family."

"Like you handled things with your daughters? With Calla? Like Grandma handled it with you?" Blair shot back. "The man molested nine—*nine* girl children and no one did a damn thing. No. One. Then you're setting the stage for him *and* your husband to do the same things to your granddaughters, nieces, and cousin's children. All because you're allowing pedophilia and predatory behavior to become the norm in this family."

"He's not a pedophile," she squawked, turning to face her sisters. "He's just sick. He's getting help. We've just been victims of a generational curse."

"Let's call a thing a thing," Blair warned. "So, I am going to say this. Stop laying this at the feet of generational curses and call it what it is—generational bad choices."

Blair let that sink in for several moments. Most of the aunts were staring at her and she could see the wheels churning in their minds. That's why they weren't putting up as much of an argument. They knew that Blair was right in taking action. She could only wish someone had done the same for them.

"Now, if you don't mind." Blair turned her back to them and moved toward the front door to slide into her shoes. "I have some living to do. None of it includes having any of you anywhere near me or my children."

"Oh, and my grandchildren, too?" Dorsey snapped.

Blair whirled to face her. "What are you talking about?"

"You petitioned the judge to give you custody of Alex, Tony, and Johnny." She took in Blair's surprised expression. "Yeah, I found out. They had to contact me at some point."

"You disregarded their words," Blair yelled. "You didn't believe them and said they were lying, just to keep a man in the house. You chose *him* over *them*. How sick is that?"

"You're taking my boys to *that* strange place?"

"You're damn straight I am. Why would I give the court the opportunity to let them back in your house? What message does it send to leave them behind? You won't let him go. What if he decides that one hole is just as good as another? So, miss me with your self-righteous indignation and anger."

"He doesn't touch little boys," Dorsey said under her breath. The rest of her aunts inched backward, giving them space.

Blair stiffened. "Listen to yourself. He doesn't touch little girls! You just confirmed that you are well aware of what he's done to them." Blair looked at her with disgust. "I'm going to see to it that they receive the help they so desperately need, since you are of the mind to let your husband, your father and uncles help themselves to the children in our family."

"But he hasn't done anything to you," she protested.

"Doesn't mean your husband didn't try, though," Blair shot back. "Where did you think he got that broken nose?" She shook her head. "Took me a week to get the blood out of my blouse. So, don't tell me what I don't know." She jabbed a finger toward her aunt. "Don't tell me that I'm being overprotective. Don't tell me that I'm being uppity because I don't associate myself with some family members. Don't bring me that bull about family comes first. Or that line about what happens here, stays here. Because all kinfolk ain't my real folks."

"And I will stand with her," Christian said, then he lowered to his knees so he was on level with their younger cousins who were standing at points between the aunts who hadn't moved an inch since Dorsey's ugly confession. "Any child that needs to speak with me or Blair …"

Blair extended her arm. "Take my hand. It's safe. We will keep you safe. You won't be hurt anymore."

"You can't just take our kids, our grandkids like that," Dorsey shouted. "It's wrong. So wrong."

"Either the State will get them, or we will," Christian said, in a calm voice, but his eyes were flashing with an anger Blair had never seen from him. "Your choice. They will come with us while you take the time to get your shit together."

Blair joined Christian on the floor, so they were both eye level with the children, but she looked up at Dorsey and said, "Yes, and see how long those men will stay with you when there are no children around."

"If any family member has touched you in your private place …" Christian looked up as Alex and Tony moved forward. "Or made you feel … uncomfortable, please …"

Blair knew she couldn't take the other kids with her right now, but she would put in motion everything needed to bring them to Durabia, along with Alex, Tony, and Johnny. She hoped Christian would be okay staying stateside until everything was in place to bring the other children to Durabia. The last thing she needed was to make it to the airport and have her aunts claim she was a kidnapper. She'd put in a call to Khalil to see if there was a space in The Castle, or maybe one of the Kings had options. Either way, she would not leave this place until every single one of them were safe. Every. Single. One.

Vicky, Darlene's daughter, tried to block the children's path.

"And if you keep them from saying something, then you are part of the problem," Christian warned.

Blair looked at her cousin Joyce's youngest daughter, whose lips trembled with an effort to speak. Joyce was Dorsey's daughter.

Blair stretched out her arms.

Tiffany didn't waste time, pulling out of her mother's hold. She ran between her siblings and straight into Blair's arms.

Blair embraced her. "It's all right. It's all right," she promised, then glanced reassuringly at a frightened little face over Tiffany's head. Little Shana closed her eyes as she inched forward and blindsided the room when she said, "Daddy said I'd be in trouble if I told …"

And so, it began.

Christian moved to Blair's side and took her hand in his. "I stand with Blair. I'll be there. I'll help with them."

"You don't even have kids," Dorsey growled, giving Christian a disdainful onceover.

"Facts," Christian countered, and his expression hardened. "But I know enough that we will keep them safe. Because you most certainly can't."

"Are you going to put them in therapy?" Blair asked with a pointed look at Joyce, then Dorsey, and Vicky. She noticed that the other aunts had tears streaming down their faces. She wanted to rush to them, hold them, and tell them everything would be all right for them, too.

"No," Blair said, answering her own question. "Because you're going to be too afraid they will spill the family secrets. And if they don't get help, they'll carry the burden of what's been done to them for the rest of their lives. Just like you do."

Christian picked up Shana from the floor. "Get help yourselves—"

"What are we supposed to tell people?" Joyce whined, hands wringing with an effort to contain her angst.

"What you really mean is what are you going to tell the men who've been abusing them?" Blair spat. "That's what you really mean."

"We don't give a damn what you tell them," Christian said between his teeth.

Blair shook her head in disdain. "You all pushed away every good man that came into your lives until you landed ones who would do the same thing to your daughters, then your granddaughters and grandsons. Kept Uncle Joe around, grandpa, and kept your husband around, knowing they was a danger to them. When will it end? Why can't it end right now?"

"Give us some time, please," Christian implored, sweeping a gaze across everyone in the room. "Then maybe we'll bring you over to Durabia for visits. I promise. Right now, it's about them."

Vicky grabbed her granddaughter, who yelped at the harsh treatment. "She's not going to say nothin'. She knows better than—"

"Look at you. So afraid of losing him," Blair snapped at her while Christian extracted the little girl from the woman's hold and held her in his arms.

"Let's make a deal," Blair challenged. "I'll take her with me for a few weeks. Just a few. Over the summer. If he leaves you because she isn't there, or if your sex life doesn't improve because he'll now be turning to you instead of using her, that should tell you plenty. Then you'll know who or what's important to him." She held out her cell. "Call him, put it on speaker phone and tell him they won't be there. Watch how hard he protests. Let us all hear it so there will be no doubt in anyone's mind."

Chapter 26

Chicago had hit a rough patch of weather and Blair was wishing for the warmth of the Durabian sun. She made a phone call to her mom before her visit with Auntie Amanda to pick her brains on where her father could be.

"Hey Mom, have you seen or talked to Dad in a while?" Blair asked, adjusting the earpiece so she could hear clearly.

"Hey B, what's wrong?" Lela said in that calming voice that usually put Blair at ease. She'd nicknamed Blair "B" early on, short for "Busy Bee" because Blair was always getting into something. Almost like the Sunshine Girl.

"I've been looking for him," Blair answered. "But he changes numbers like he changes girlfriends."

Lela laughed so hard she almost caught the hiccups. "I haven't spoken to him in over a year. Why are you looking for him? Did you ask your brother?"

Blair sighed and shifted in the driver's seat, "Not yet. They're putting me through some paces over there and I need him to sign an important form. I would have asked Uncle Terry, but they said my father has to do it."

Her mother was silent for a moment. "Well, I'll see what I can do, baby girl, but I won't make any promises. I'd give you away myself if I could."

"I know, Ma. Thanks for trying. Love you."

"Love you too, B."

Blair's stepfather, Eric Senior, had been in and out of her life since she was a baby. Now, she didn't know where he was and hadn't spoken to him in years. She often thought that if she had a consistent father figure, things would have been different. Maybe she would have gone straight to college after high school and stayed on the right tack, instead of wanting to live the fast life.

It still hurt that Devon had abandoned her as a baby. Sometimes she kicked herself because as a grown woman, she believed she should be over it. She used to watch movies about fathers loving their daughters and the tears would overwhelm her, followed by questions. *Why not me? Why didn't he choose me?*

Blair always wanted to know what it felt like to be a princess to a king. The way her daughters looked at their father at one time. For all of his faults, Antonio was a damn good father at first, despite always being an asshole of a husband.

She was still grateful to her stepfather for stepping in when he could, but it wasn't enough for her. Her mother then remarried, and the new guy was actually a good man, a good husband for her mom. Blair loved him and definitely considered him family, but by the time she hit those teenage years she figured it was too late for a father and daughter relationship.

Now her three children looked at Hassan as their father. He had taken the role of surrogate father even more seriously than their biological one. For her, the stability and love she hadn't experienced was important for her children. That's why she had to do her part. But the days were passing, and they were cutting it too close.

She had to find her biological father. Her issues with trust all started with him.

* * *

Blair settled into a seat across from Auntie Amanda on the beige leather couch. Auntie Amanda had a golden complexion, short wavy hair, and flawless skin. They could talk without interruption because the children were knocked out in their rooms upstairs after a full day of shopping for clothes as part of their transition to living with her, and then Christian, in Durabia.

"I love Devon," Amanda said, clasping her hands tightly as if she were praying. "We've had an interesting relationship over the years. Only when I stopped holding him to "my" standard of who he should be and what he should do in life, could I love him unconditionally. I never appreciated how he treated his children. That's why we—Ellena, Melissa, and I—stayed in his children's lives even when the rest of the family didn't."

Blair gave her the side eye, but clamped down on her comments about his negligence.

"No, I'm not trying to make excuses for him, but there's something I've come to realize," Amanda said, looking at Blair, who bit her bottom lip trying to remain silent. "You see, my brother is one of those 'add on' dudes."

Blair opened her mouth to speak but Amanda held up a hand to hold off the query. "Let me explain what I mean by 'add on'. Once, I had to cook an entire meal—about eight or nine dishes—and get them to the table at the same time. Let me tell you I almost lost my natural mind."

The tension in the room eased when Blair chuckled.

"So, don't expect me to ever do a full Thanksgiving dinner," Auntie Amanda said. "I'll bring the four-cheese mac & cheese. I'll bring the sweet potato pie or peach cobbler. What that means is that I'm an "add on" cook. Not because I can't do a thing, but because it's not in my heart and true ability to perform the mechanics well enough to do the *whole* thing."

One thing about Auntie Amanda, she always had a point. Blair had a hard time understanding this one and shifted in the seat, waiting

"In that, my brother is the same way," she continued. "He can't deal with the child unless he's with the mother, so he missed out on raising the children before this one he has with his current wife. Now a couple of disclaimers here, wife number two was a volatile relationship. They are both good people, but definitely not good together. But when he was in that relationship, he was there for his daughter in every way—the "add on" way because he didn't have to do anything but provide money and have a presence."

Amanda shifted the empty shot glass in front of her, then simply held it in her hands. "And when the marriage ended, he tried to keep that presence for a hot minute, but not altogether too hard. I'm being as honest about this as I see it."

Blair poured her a shot of Disaronno, an Italian liqueur, and settled in for the rest of the story.

"My mother didn't encourage him to act like a normal dad. Instead she found every reason he shouldn't be involved with his children. He didn't need much incentive to back away, being a mama's boy. She wasn't keen on sharing his time and money, so she supported his flimsy excuses. Does it make it right that he did? He hadn't become *that man* yet."

"And that is unfortunate for him and his children," Blair added in a sour tone.

"True. Girlfriend number …" Auntie Amanda shook her head. "Lost count, but he didn't have children with all of them—just three-and-a-half children in all, Lela was a sweetheart with none of the baggage and anger of some of the others."

Regret shone from her eyes as she said, "When that relationship failed, he drifted and missed out on raising a beautiful, intelligent daughter who's become a surgical nurse, and has three children, a soon-to-be ex, and a man in the wings who loves her dearly."

Blair sighed and said with a slight smile. "You are talking about me and my mom."

"Yes, sweetie, and Lela really was a sweetheart, and still is today but no, I'm not making excuses here; I'm stating what I believe. And I truly love you like no other and realize that his abandonment has caused you a lot of pain." Amanda placed a hand over Blair's and held it there for a moment.

"I had a talk with Christian on Father's Day, because he was hurting too." Auntie Amanda downed another shot of liquor, then slid the glass away. "How drunk do I have to be to have the rest of this conversation?"

"Auntie, you know you love this stuff," Blair teased, grinning. "Had me hooked too, until I found Moscato."

"True," she said chuckling, then all the humor left her face. "Everything I've said to you, I explained to him and I told him that his father was pretty much the same. Christian's father left because his mother did not approve of an interracial relationship, same way his father left five children behind. But that's another subject for another time. In the end, he didn't know how to navigate a relationship without there being any sexual ties to the mother. He couldn't handle the responsibility of building a relationship with his son on his own."

"I definitely want to hear more about that." Blair was grateful Christian was a better man than his father. He had spent the entire day working with the Kings to expedite the paperwork required to bring all of the children to Durabia. Khalil had them at The Castle with her mother and Christian's mother watching out for them. Teamwork.

"Now back to my knucklehead brother," she said with a weary sigh. "Christian has felt some kind of way about my brother due to the fact that he equates his actions to being the same as his father's. I told him that my brother—at age fifty-five—has finally grown into the father his other children would have loved to see." She raised her glass. "Lesson learned, and I'm so proud that he's stepped up in this regard, but I'm praying he'll bridge the gap with all of his children at some point. Even if he can't have a relationship with them, they need to understand … why."

Blair poured Auntie Amanda another shot. She laughed and lifted it in mock salute. "So, to men who don't understand that their presence is required irrespective of the relationship with the mother, or whether they pay child support. None of that adult shit matters to the child. Some may realize that it's never too late to become the father he should have been. And they'll show up when you need them most or maybe not showing up is a better thing overall."

Auntie Amanda clasped Blair's hand in her own. "I need you to release your father because you've been subconsciously holding on, and it's keeping you from moving forward. Forgive him if you can, and if not, just try to understand. Life isn't always neatly packaged, with instructions or a list of frequently asked questions. People are people doing the best they can, even if it all amounts to shit."

This time, it was Blair who downed a shot.

Chapter 27

Hassan gathered his things and prepared to leave the hotel for the Durabia airport. He had continued making arrangements as though he hadn't noticed the car that had been trailing him since first thing that morning.

"You take this document, have Taj sign it. And have Fahim at the United States Embassy put his seal on these. I'll go to Hani, and then we will meet up at the airport. Deal?"

"Deal," Akeem answered.

Haleem, his other brother, glanced at the pages. "You know Sheikh Hakim just touched down and his daughter is with him. And Sheikh Yasin landed last night, his daughter is here, too. You're getting married today."

"To whom is a different story."

Hassan had a sinking feeling in the pit of his belly. "Call the airport, reserve a private room until after two o'clock. If it has to be a prayer room, so be it."

"Let's hope her plane makes it in on time," Akeem said.

"Brother, you sure did pick a great time to break from tradition," Haleem teased with a grin.

Akeem nodded. "Father is going to be spitting mad."

"That may be true, but I know I will be happy. And that means Sabah is back on the market."

Haleem's smile widened. "And that means, I might actually have a chance."

"And what is the real reason you want to help me with getting married to Blair?" Hassan said with a hearty chuckle.

"Oh, come on, brother. You know Sabah's father is not going to marry her to you if you are with Blair first." Haleem shook his head. "His daughter, second to a non-believer. Not in this lifetime."

"True, but that means you have a shot at Sabah now," Hassan said. "And she is a delight."

A dreamy smile curved his brother's lips. "That she is."

* * *

The prayer room at the airport had been transformed with an array of colorful flowers and a row of ladder-back chairs for the few guests that would be present. Hassan was staying hidden there while his brothers handled the rest of the paperwork on his end. But Hassan's connection at the embassy warned him that the *biological* father stipulation was a solid requirement that they couldn't get around.

All eyes turned to Dro who grimaced and said, "Not yet."

"We have less than thirty minutes," Hassan reminded them.

When Blair landed, she had been reluctant to have Raheim transport the children to her home where Fatimah was keeping an eye on Blair's kids. Hassan convinced her that it was best, considering this marriage attempt might turn out to be volatile.

"I know, but his plane is still taxiing on the tarmac," Daron said.

Hassan checked his watch. "He won't make it here in time."

"Who?" Blair asked, gaze narrowing on him.

He embraced her warmly. "Give it a minute, my love."

"I have an idea," Dro said to Daron. "Find out what gate they're pulling into."

Hassan perked up and so did his brothers. "What do you have in mind?"

"Let's make moves." Dro scanned the group. "Call for them to bring one of those mobile carts."

"Actually, we'll need two of them." Haleem dashed away and came back riding shotgun in one cart. He stalked back into the room and announced, "They're sending another one from Terminal B. It's going to take about ten to fifteen minutes."

"Let's move people," Dro commanded. "Hassan, Blair, and Kamran get in the cart. Khalil, Christian, Hiram, Daron and I will make it on foot."

"They need two Muslim witnesses," Akeem said. "Two male family members. The last part of the requirement is on his way in."

"What other requirement?" Blair asked while they hurried to their makeshift transport.

When they stepped inside, the driver of the cart took off at breakneck speed.

The corners of Hassan's eyes crinkled. "I did not want to tell you just in case he didn't show."

Blair tilted her head to the side, confusion etched in her face as she peered at him. "Who didn't show?"

"Be patient, my love." They were pulling into the gate when he finally answered, "Your father."

"Of course, my father would come," she scoffed, giving a dismissive wave. "He—"

Every ounce of color drained from her face as she nearly slid off the seat. "What? Why? How?"

"Marriage requires the physical presence of your father," Hassan explained. "If he is alive, and his signature on this form."

Blair's lips barely moved as she said, "Eric Senior is my father."

"His name is not on your birth certificate, love," Hassan said in a quiet tone. "They needed your *biological* father."

She swallowed hard and seemed almost ready to faint. "I haven't seen him in thirty something years."

"I know," he whispered, taking her hand in his.

"Why would he come now?" she said through her teeth.

"Because you needed him."

"I needed him growing up," she cried, gripping Hassan's hand so tight he had to catch his breath. "Where was he? Where was he?"

"I know," he whispered, and his heart went out to her. "I should have told you of my plans. We searched for him and I didn't tell you because if we couldn't find him, I didn't want you to be disappointed all over again. You've been hurt so much, and it would have killed me to be the source of more pain."

Dro tapped his watch and Hassan sighed, but shook his head. He was not going to rush this along. He had planned for their marriage to happen in a way that she didn't have to lay eyes on her father. Devon would have said "I give this woman" at the time he was supposed to, but from an obscure place in the room, and then leave without a scene. Their deadline and the flight delays had changed all that.

The tall man with a warm brown complexion several shades darker than Blair, who stood a few feet from them almost cringed under Blair's glare.

"I cannot give you anything or say anything," Devon said, keeping a little distance between them. "To make up for things that I did wrong. To make things right. All I have is now... *this* day.... You are the one thing in my life I did right. I am not deserving of your forgiveness or understanding. I was the adult in the situation and I failed. I failed myself and I failed you."

"You are correct," she snarled, chest heaving in an effort to contain her emotions. "You can't. What about me? Why couldn't you love me? What did I do that I didn't deserve your love?" She fell against Hassan's chest, sobbing.

"When I couldn't love myself, Blair, how could I make room for anything or anyone else? I was wrong and I will forever be sorry for that. You deserve better, better than me."

"Your father's guards just cleared the area," Daron warned.

Hassan tightened his hold on Blair and spoke with regret coloring his voice. "There won't be a wedding today. She needs time to process her feelings."

Daron groaned and shot back, "But–"

"I know. I know," Hassan conceded and there was a collective groan from the group. "Right now, she needs time, more than I need to rush her into this marriage."

Blair pulled away from his chest, searching his eyes for a moment. She seemed confident that he would do what was in her best interest, and that included forgoing the marriage altogether because she was in no condition to handle her emotions plus a momentous occasion.

The disappointment he felt was so profound he had to take several deep breaths to find center. She came first, especially now that their family had expanded. The children needed her to be the best version of herself. With a hand on her arm, Hassan guided Blair and the group back to the prayer room.

When they entered, Hassan murmured. "It's all right, we don't have to do this now."

"Love yourself, baby girl," Devon said, interrupting. "That brass ring standing right in front of you, grab onto it. It's your turn now. Love yourself enough to love him." He nodded toward Hassan and said to her, "Go on now. Do what's best for you."

Hassan caught her cheek against the warm wall of his hand.

"We don't have to do this Blair. If you need time—"

"No, no, we can … I'm all right." Blair glanced at Devon, who silently stood watching.

In the passage, Daron glanced over Akeem's shoulder. "They just cleared security."

"Are you ready?" Kamran asked.

"Yes, Sheikh," Blair said, wiping her face with the tissues Hassan handed over.

"Let's do this in reverse," Khalil said as Hakeem held out the documents for everyone to sign while he said, "Who gives this woman?"

Dro, Daron, Jai, and Devon said they did.

Khalil passed Jai his pen and squared his shoulders as he looked first to Hassan, then to Blair. "Do you take this woman?"

"Yes." Hassan's tone was calm and confident.

"Do you take this man?"

Blair inhaled deeply and with a tremulous smile on her face, answered, "Yes."

No sooner had the word slipped past her lips than Hassan took her face in his hands like a challis and kissed her hard and deep. Blair practically sobbed against his mouth as she returned the kiss.

A few chuckles and whistles of approval sounded as Vikkas said, "Are you going to let her up for air?"

Hassan opened one eye, then the other as he finally pulled away and said, "Not if I can help it."

"I now pronounce you man and wife." Khalil sighed, then smiled.

"Now, let's start from the beginning.

In the middle of the speech, several beefy men wearing dishdashas flung the door open and burst into the room.

Dro and Daron rushed toward the doorway, but Hassan held up his hand and said, "No, let it happen."

The men separated Hassan from Blair and carted him off like last week's luggage. Dro and Daron were spitting mad as they holstered their weapons.

Wearing a delighted grin, Khalil said, "We'll be right behind you."

Chapter 28

"Married," Yousef roared, and the sound bounced off of every wall in the house, from the foyer, cloakroom, en suite guest room, storage room, completely fitted kitchen, maid's room on the ground floor, to generous sized bedrooms and a family room on the first floor. Anyone standing in the fully landscaped garden that boasted a private pool probably heard him as well.

"That makes her first wife," Akeem said, as his brother nudged him into silence.

Hassan leveled a gaze at his father, whose anger was so tangible it would frighten the most courageous of people. "Yes, it does. Blair is my first wife. My only wife. There will be no others."

The combination of natural light and the white décor in the spacious living room made their surroundings extremely bright. At the far end of the room, the family of the prospective brides watched, aghast, while

Blair was escorted to Hassan's side with Khalil, Dro, and Daron flanking her sides and back.

"I do not understand you," Yousef cried. "You know how I feel about this mixed marriage. Mixed religion. Mixed race. Mixed and messed up all the way. You defied me."

"I could still marry Sabah and Imani as second and third wives," Hassan stated, trying to hold back a smile.

Blair tensed, but he stroked her hand, urging her to let the scenario play out.

Yousef's gaze flicked in Blair's direction. "But it requires the consent of that, that …"

"Careful father," Hassan warned. "That is *my wife*—my *first* wife you're talking about. And I will not stand for her to be insulted"

Yousef flinched and sank onto the white leather couch, giving Hassan's words serious thought. "Will she consent to the marriage of Sabah and Imani?"

"I do not have an answer for that," Hassan answered. "Why don't you ask my wife, instead of alienating her."

Yousef blanched at the words "my wife," lifted his chin and looked down his nose at Blair. "It is already arranged that he marries Sabah and Imani to join our families. This is tradition."

Blair simply looked at him, remaining silent so long that Yousef squirmed.

"And?" Blair prompted, and it took everything within Hassan not to smile.

"And that is all," he said, his tone hard. "He will marry them. You will consent. And—"

"I will?" She glanced at Khalil, then Dro, Daron, and finally Hassan, who all wore smirks that signaled the answer they knew she would give.

Even Fatimah gave an approving nod.

She met Yousef's gaze with a straight face. "No, I do not consent for Hassan Ali Khan to marry any other woman. And *that* is all."

A collective gasp came from where the brides-to-be and their families watched.

Yousef gripped the edge of the chair. Fire shot from his eyes when he looked at Hassan. "You have ruined me," he roared.

"Father, Haleem is more than willing to fulfill the terms of the arranged marriage. You are not ruined. You have more than enough sons to complete this family pairing."

"They prefer you," Yousef countered, but his voice had lost some of its edge. "The daughters are excited to become your wives."

"People in hell prefer ice water." Hassan tipped one brow. "That does not mean they will get what they desire."

"No, he didn't go there," Shaz whispered to Daron and Dro, who both nodded. "My mother always said that one when she wanted to put me in check."

"Hell? You use that word?" Yousef snapped. "She is influencing you. You will be stripped of your inheritance."

"I understand." Hassan didn't balk as expected. This angered Yousef even more.

"She will not live off our family's money," he asserted, a scowl marrying his features.

"She is a surgical nurse at Durabia Medical and has the support of both the Kings of the Castle and their Knights. Not to mention she has multiple sponsorships in her financial portfolio. Blair Swanson Khan has her own money. And I have no need for your money."

Arms folded, Hassan continued, "After I fulfill the terms of my new position at the Durabian Embassy—thanks to your machinations that will cost your friends their jobs—I will be entering medical school to become a doctor like Jaidev of the Indian line of the Maharaj family. An honorable profession. And maybe, just maybe, I will be the one who figures out why Mother's illness still persists."

Fatimah clasped a hand to her heart as tears streamed down her face. The joyful vibes rolling from her filled him with so much happiness.

Yousef stood and moved closer to his son. "Is she at least going to convert to Islam?"

"No, Father," Hassan answered. "That is not a requirement for her to be my wife. I am the one who is required to love, respect, honor, and cherish her. Religion has no bearing on that." He pressed a kiss to Blair's hand, then they turned, ready to follow Khalil and the Kings out of the residence. He shared a knowing glace with his brothers who nodded.

"My son ..." Fatimah began.

"Yes, mother." His gaze went to Imani and Sabah, who sat on the long white couch with their families as they watched the drama play out.

"Blair ..."

"Yes, ma'am."

"Do you love him?" she asked just above a whisper. "Do you truly love my son?"

"Oh yes. I do," she answered, and she meant it with her entire heart. "I trust him. I respect him. Those mean more to me than ever. He has demonstrated what a real man is about. And while I won't convert to Islam, I will promise to make an effort to understand and respect the religion that is the foundation of what my husband believes."

"You have my blessing, even if you do not have his." She tipped her head in Yousef's direction. "I will open my dowry and it is yours."

The silence behind those words brought another level of tension to the room.

"If you love him, you will convert," Yousef growled, breathing heavily.

"Love does not require that kind of sacrifice," Blair countered. "And if I can convert simply because you require it, and not because I desire, is it truly a conversion or simply an act? My ancestors were already forced to give up their religion once."

"And that religion was Islam," he spat as his skin flushed with anger.

"Could be," she tossed back. "But given the way religion has been used as a weapon on women and people of color, why would I embrace Islam. Especially since you're presenting a *fine example* of what it is to be a Muslim, sir."

Fatimah closed her eyes tight and grimaced.

Vikkas nudged Jai, whose jaw had dropped as Khalil gave an appreciative nod.

Khalil whispered, "And therein lies the truth of things."

"This is not a religious thing," Yousef said through his teeth, putting a heated glare on Khalil. "He is going against our culture in taking a woman who is a nonbeliever, and who will not convert."

"I'm surrounded by Kings, Queens, and Knights," Blair said. "I'm wearing a tunic and I'm fully covered. Didn't you just say that my ancestors were Muslim? And here I am, on Muslim land, in a Muslim kingdom, married to a Muslim man. How much of a return to my ancestors' culture do I need to make?"

Fatimah's eyes opened wide, followed by an ear-to-ear smile that her husband didn't miss.

Yousef finally sighed as the moments passed without a rejoinder from him. Finally, he said, "It seems that my …" He swallowed. "Daughter-in-law is as formidable as her aunt."

Blair released a tight smile, while Yousef let out a long, slow breath. To Fatimah, he said, "We will plan a celebration in a weeks' time. And I will meet with the Hakim and Yasin families and arrange with Akeem and Haleem, unless they wish for something different too?"

"No father," Akeem said with a pointed look toward his brother, Haleem, who smiled at him. "I will happily take Imani as my first wife."

"And I will take Sabah," Haleem said, glancing toward the fleshy girl who nodded vigorously. "If she will have me."

Her parents smiled, seeming both ill-at-ease and relieved despite the unexpected turn of events.

"If we later wish to marry a nonbeliever," Akeem continued with a confident smile, "We will address that accordingly."

Hassan signaled for his brothers to pipe down on their obvious elation.

"Is there something I should know?" Yousef said.

Akeem gave a sheepish grin. "I have had a crush on Imani ever since she was a little girl. She has always wanted to be my wife but agreed to the marriage her father arranged."

Yousef scanned the smiling face of his wife. "How did I not know this?"

"There are things a son tells his mother," Fatimah said with a smile. "That he would never share with his father. Especially one with such a hard head."

Chapter 29

"What are you doing?" Salimah stormed into the office. The pale-blue wall behind the metal desk was covered with certificates and awards.

Zaina flinched, pulled the paperwork from in front of Blair, and held it out. "Firing her."

"On what grounds?" Salimah demanded, leaning on the black file cabinet as though she needed something to hold her up.

Blair wasn't sure if Salimah respected her, but by the tone it seemed at least she realized that Blair was needed here.

"Insubordination," Zaina shot back.

"You cannot be serious," Salimah snapped. "Not only is she the most requested surgical nurse in the hospital, Dr. Maharaj asked that she start training the other nurses." She read the documents Zaina had compiled, her expression registering everything from disbelief to anger as she skimmed the pages. "So, I am having a hard time matching your experiences with her with what everyone else is saying."

Blair leaned back in the chair. "Yes, I'd like to understand that myself. Let it make sense."

Silence ensued for a few moments, and Zaina's face went through a range of expressions as if she was unable to cope with being second-guessed.

"All the other doctors, nurses, and lab technicians speak very highly of Blair." Salimah straightened and continued, "It's a little suspect that the only people who seem to have an issue with her happen to be you and your friends."

Zaina mulled that over a moment. "Well, maybe we can consider this a warning. If she can keep her attitude in check, then—"

"Do you know what?" Blair said, standing. "Since I can't guarantee that I won't have an attitude, whatever that means, let's consider today my last day here."

Zaina perked up, obviously elated. "You're quitting?"

"I have options," Blair said. "Jaidev Maharaj Germaine is opening a healing center here in Durabia. I have a standing invitation to join his employ. With my business sponsorships, I now own nine businesses that will float me until the center is open. So yes, I'll get out of this woman's hair, and she can stop focusing on me and actually do her job."

"We accept your resignation," Zaina said with a haughty lift of her chin. "I'll have security escort you from the building."

"Absolutely not," Salimah countered, her green eyes flashing with fire. "I have the final say. And we are *not* firing her."

"No, she's right," Blair admitted, sliding her purse strap onto her shoulder. "We both can't work here, and she's saved me the trouble of making the rounds."

"Making the rounds? What does that mean," the director asked. "All I know is that I do not wish to explain to the surgeons why our top nurse is missing."

Blair extracted a document from her pocket, folded it, then creased the corner before tearing it in half. One half, she threw on the desk and securely tucked the other into her bra

"What's this, millions of dollars?" Zaina scoffed, flickering a glance at the writing. "Your wish list?"

Blair smiled and replied, "No, actually, I suggested to several doctors that we should have a wing dedicated to survivors of sexual abuse, rape, sex trafficking, and domestic violence. Doctor Earmen and Doctor Maharaj said if I could raise the funds, they'll put it in the pipeline immediately." She gestured to the paper and the women's gazes followed her movements. "That's millions of dollars as a start from my family members, and the Kings and Knights of the Castle as well. I'm supposed to have a private audience with Sheikh Kamran this evening after dinner. He showed interest in offering his support for my idea when I emailed him. He didn't specify it had to be for this hospital, so ..." She shrugged, giving them both a megawatt smile. "I'm certain Jaidev would welcome me—and this plan—with open arms. And on that note, deuces." She stood, smiled, and gave them the sideways peace sign. "No need for security to see me to my locker. There's nothing in there. After the first few run-ins with you, I never felt secure enough to bring anything personal."

Salimah blocked her path to the door. "What are your conditions for staying?"

"Why would I remain in a hostile work environment?" Blair shot back. "Where's the fun in that?"

"Suppose I make it less hostile ..." Her penciled eyebrow quirked upward.

Blair leaned the file cabinet. "I don't understand."

"If I remove the element that is causing the issue ..."

Blair glanced over her shoulder and took in Zaina's bland expression, which meant she was oblivious to what the conversation actually meant. "Well, I could stay a while longer, at least through my original employment contract date, but the idea of having my own center is now at the forefront of my mind. Maybe Jaidev will think a franchise of sorts might be in my best interest."

"But you'll remain here in the interim?"

Blair gave it a few moments of thought, but she already knew her answer. "Yes, if the conditions are substantially better than they have been since I arrived. And I mean across the board. Also, I'll have to get my husband's insight on everything, but ..."

The director turned, smiled at Zaina, and said, "I'll have security escort you out."

* * *

"Well, of course my wife would love to continue working for the hospital but in a totally different capacity," Hassan advised, a day later as they sat across from the director.

Salimah glanced at the document. "But her contract means she's supposed to be here six days a week."

"Yes, but that was prior to this." He slid the termination letter that Blair managed to hang onto across the desk.

"Oh, that was a mistake," she said pushing the document back toward him.

Hassan leaned back in the chair. "Her lawyer says otherwise."

"Lawyer?" The director of nursing let her head swivel between Hassan and Blair.

"Yes. Vikkas, a member of the royal family, is handling the matter, but we thought we would feel things out and see if we could come up with a compromise without involving him. You know, a gentleman's agreement of sorts—in writing. She already bypassed filing a suit for a hostile work environment."

"That doesn't fly here," Salimah said with a pointed look at Hassan. "Durabia doesn't have anything in place for that."

"She signed her contract in the United States because the headquarters for recruitment is there. The contract is American based, and so was she at the time of the signing. She could have easily brought a case on that alone."

"But we would like to avoid that," Blair said, giving Hassan's hand a gentle squeeze.

Salimah's eyes skimmed the office then returned to Blair. "What are your terms?"

"I'm on rotation only three times a week." Blair said and carefully watched Salimah's reaction go to straight panic.

"But—"

"Three. And I'd do seminars and workshops to train the other nurses."

"But you haven't been here long enough for that," Salimah huffed.

"I've been here long enough to figure out where improvement is needed," Blair fired back.

Salimah sank back in her seat, muttering to herself. "Four days," Salimah offered.

"Three," Blair insisted. "You're going in the wrong direction."

Sitting up straight, Salimah said, "Final offer."

Blair didn't bother to answer.

Salimah glanced at the paperwork and rubbed her temples. "The doctors will have my hide."

"Better yours than my wife's," Hassan said dryly.

Salimah sent him a soft glare. "That's not funny."

"It is, from where I'm sitting," Hassan said, taking Blair's hand in his. "The doctors are her concern as well. If she's doing the training, they will have a team of nurses, not just one who they request all the time. This is what is called a win-win."

Chapter 30

After Hassan found out the shady work that Hani at the Durabian Embassy had done on Yousef's behalf, he relieved him of his duties and took over not only his job, but the department as well. The cherry-haired lady who gave up the scoop became his personal assistant. Equally Fahim was sent back to the states, packing. One of his first, slightly personal, actions was to set an alert for Antonio's name on any flights into Durabia, so he couldn't pull a repeat of his little surprise. They would take care of him in a different way this time.

After a few weeks, Hassan's foresight paid off. Once Antonio had slipped into the country, the Rehabilitation Center where his mother had been admitted was where that private detail tracked him. Hassan made his way immediately to the center, and he had a burly, armed entourage trailing behind.

"Take him," Hassan commanded the moment they cleared the car.

The guards moved forward, gripped Antonio under the arms, and prepared to perp walk him to the only jail center in Durabia. That would begin the process for deporting him—and not to the United States this time.

"You can't keep me from seeing my mother," Antonio roared, struggling against his restraints. "What the hell do you think you're doing."

"Putting you on notice," he said, moving closer. "See, you're in *my hood* now. Placing your hands on a royal is an offense."

"She ain't no damn royal," he protested. "She's just Blair from a block in Jeffrey Manor."

"Her aunt is married to the Sheikh of Durabia. The highest position in this country. Blair is related to that ruler by marriage which counts for something around these parts. And what you did to her was enough to ban you from ever setting foot in this place again." Hassan took a step toward Antonio. "See, in other places, you would disappear into the desert and we'd teach you all about respect. Be grateful, because if my uncle didn't have shackles on my actions, I would mop the palace grounds with you."

"It's floor," one of the guards corrected.

"He knows what I mean." Hassan said, keeping his focus on Antonio. "If you ever lay a hand to her again, my uncle will just have to be upset. You are not going to play my wife like a bass drum."

"It's actually—"

Hassan silenced the guard with a look. "He knows what I mean." Then his gaze locked on Antonio again. "You will never lay eyes on her again."

"I don't know how you are going to manage that," Antonio snarled. "We have children together, there's no getting around that fact. She's my—"

"Ex-wife and *my* wife. Your ex because you didn't see her value. Ex, because you didn't want to pay to help your children—all because you do not control her any longer. Not her body. Not her mind. You have taken enough."

A crowd of people leaving the center stood a ways back, watching.

A flood of color darkened Antonio's tanned skin. "You can't keep me from my kids."

"Actually, I could, but Blair does not desire that." Hassan was still in awe of his huge new family and the ease with which all the children accepted him into their lives, despite what they'd been through. "And she accepted your attempt at dodging child support by agreeing to your request to terminate your parental rights. That's a fatherly low even I have never heard of. So all things considered that document—termination is fully in affect."

Antonio tried to break away from the guards, shouting, "What about my mother and sister? You can't stop me from seeing them."

"You didn't come here to see your mother. You came to terrorize *my* wife. By law, I have every right to exercise *my* husband's rights if I feel like my family is being harassed. Trust me that's deadly ground you walk on."

Antonio squinted, tilting his head. "Is that a threat?"

Hassan straightened his tie before he took a step closer to Antonio. "Certainly not. I make blood vows, again very dangerous ground you walk on."

My family is here. My mother—-"

"Grows weary of you. You've already worn out your welcome with one visit to them. They will return to America in another few weeks, once your mother is fully recovered, so that won't be a problem. Unless, of course, they choose to remain in Durabia."

Antonio yelled, "They said all you ragheads were serpents and that we shouldn't let you close to our women."

"A serpent? Antonio, let me ask you this, if the serpent came close enough to seduce your woman, where were you?" Hassan smiled.

"Don't blame me for your failures."

Antonio's face flushed a deeper red. "My failures?"

"Now let me tell you how this is going to work," Hassan said, moving in closer. "You want to see your children and have some type of presence in their lives? Video chats every other night and you'd better not miss a single one if you're serious, or I will terminate that possibility. Then you will save your coins and I will match whatever you manage to scrape up for airfare for you to visit here twice a year."

"But you have a private plane," Antonio protested, shrugging the guards away to no avail.

"Yes, I have a private plane—emphasis on the pronoun 'I'." Hassan smirked. "And you are not going to be anywhere on it. Economy will be your best friend. And when you are here, you will stay in a hotel far from where Blair lives, and visit with your children in a supervised setting. All under security escort."

"They're my children," he shouted. "How are you going to dictate what I do?"

"Because I can. Because it's right. You didn't appreciate her or them when you had ample opportunity. Now, you will have to earn your time with them."

"All of this so you can slide up in my wife—"

"Ex-wife. Remember?" Hassan shot back. "Ex marks the spot where you … fucked up. You left her open for a better man to pick up where you never left off."

"And you're that better man?"

"You had better believe it." Hassan smiled, then signaled for them to put Antonio in the car. "And I'm going to make sure she never doubts it."

Chapter 31

Blair took the microphone off the pole and moved into the audience. "I'd like to welcome you all to Durabia Medical Hospital. I'm not here to teach you what you didn't learn in school. I'm here to teach you what they failed to make you aware of. No textbooks here. No teachers correcting your mistakes. Welcome to the real world."

Murmurs rippled through the audience of people of various ethnic backgrounds.

"Working as a nurse, actually applying the things you learned, is a whole different ball game. You'll have to become conscious of your surroundings at all times. You'll have to be more sensitive to patients, their pain, and their care. Simple things matter."

Blair put aside her notes that she had carefully created over a month. She had never been so nervous. Hassan had helped, but he constantly said to keep things simple. The same way he had with a brief, but wonderful honeymoon trip to Shadow Bay, an east coast American town. She smiled at the memories and his advice. *Keep it simple.*

"How many parents do we have in here?"

Blair watched as all but ten of the hands in the room shot up.

"Then most of you remember the moment the nurse or doctor put your baby in your arms for the first time, yes?' Blair said as she nodded, and some of them did too. "After counting fingers and toes I couldn't sing to save my life, but I made promises. I was their first friend and the best one. They could always trust me with anything. Stories every night and hugs and…all the things I never had when we were growing up. Trust… safety… peace. My mother was a working woman and had to keep her focus on making sure we had a roof over our heads, food on the table, and clothes on our backs. But in our world, with our children, we'd slay any dragon, any monster on four legs or two. Right?"

Blair nodded again as she watched the nurses like a tapestry in all colors and creeds nodding at one another.

"Now imagine those sleepless nights," she directed them. "Your child is burning up or maybe they're teenagers or an adult and you get *The Call.* You get to a hospital and there are strangers running about rattling off stats and chattering in medical terminology. You get to the desk and it dawns on you. You broke your promise. You can't keep them safe. You can't fix it. You can't make the pain or the sickness or the fear go away." She placed a hand over her heart. "Then it really hits you. The one perfect thing you ever did in your life, this piece of your soul, and you have to hand it over to a stranger and say the four most frightening words in the world. "'Please, help my child.'" She allowed those words to settle in. "Maybe it's you who needs help and it's five words… 'I don't want to die' or two … 'I'm scared'."

A hush fell over the room as some of the women dabbed at their eyes.

Maybe you are a woman sitting on a bed in the Labor and Delivery unit. You can hear babies crying or the lullaby signaling that one was just born. You're sitting there with swollen breasts and a hole growing in the middle of your soul. Your arms are empty because your baby was stillborn. Are there even words for something like that?"

The gasped that echoed in the room, signaled her point had been made.

"That is what your patients are feeling," Blair said. "It is the unending nightmare their families experience on a daily basis. Who are you? You're the nurse. You are the buffer. You are hope personified."

Blair glanced around, moving further down the aisle.

"Our work is not for the faint of heart," she warned. "Patients want to be treated as if you were the patient. As if your loved ones were the patient. You are angels in your patients' eyes. You're the hero in your patients' eyes. You help save lives for a living." Blair glanced over her shoulder at the screen and read the words that were displayed. "The great Maya Angelou wrote, "As nurses, we have the opportunity to heal the heart, mind, soul, and body of our patients, their families and ourselves." Blair walked back to the center in front of the podium. "They may not remember your name, but they'll never forget the way you made them feel. Welcome to the front lines, Nurses. If you are ready, then let us begin."

The nurses applauded as Blair left the auditorium to be greeted by her handsome husband at the door.

"You were amazing," Hassan whispered as he kissed her cheek, then led her to the blue Rolls Royce.

"It's a powerful feeling to be walking in your purpose," Blair said as she slid into the passenger seat. She waited until he was behind the wheel to continue. "I was thinking that before now, so many of these women wouldn't have been able to do this work. They weren't allowed to live their best lives."

"Caging their talents, also cages that country's progress," Hassan said, turning in the direction of a restaurant not too far from the mansion where all of her cousins were now situated with her mother. "My uncle is very much against that. Your aunt is leading that charge."

Blair was so proud of Auntie—correction, Sheikha Ellena. And she so wanted to find a way for Auntie Amanda to be in Durabia as well.

"That's why I wanted to be here," she confessed. "To serve, encourage, and inspire, but to also serve notice. There's a man who's in the highest office in America who has been accused of unspeakable things against women, children, and those who did business with him." Blair took in a deep breath, then continued, "Take. Take. Take. No consequences for their actions. Impregnate without impunity, even through rape, and the women must keep their child regardless. So much of that is wrong."

"With you and Sheikha Ellena at the helm, his days—and men like him, are numbered."

Hassan reached out for her hand and she smiled and said, "I'm happy to know that the Kings and Knights are working to make a difference in the world. I like them."

"Yes, they're all right," he said with a chuckle, then pulled to a stop at the sidewalk and switched off the engine. Hassan held the door, first to the car, then the restaurant.

The children, Christian, Hassan's mother, and his brothers and their new wives were seated at a long table in the center. His father was not present, but that was all right.

"We're making an impact as well," Hassan said, "Teaching the children to speak love even when their voices are being overpowered by others."

Blair smiled. "You're right. You can never underestimate the power of small changes. It's still progress."

With an affectionate gaze, she studied Alex, Tony, Johnny, and Shana who had flourished in their new environment. Blair lowered herself next to her sunshine girl and squeezed Hassan's fingers. She was grateful for the love that now surrounded her and that her tomorrows were filled with the promise of better things to come.

About the Authors

J. S. Cole is a Chicago native who has a proven track record in the medical industry. Her debut novel, Lady of Jeffrey Manor is part of the Knights of the Castle Series. She resides in South Holland with her wonderful husband and three amazing children where she is working on her next book.

www.authorjscole.com

Naleighna Kai is the USA TODAY, Essence®, and national bestselling and award-winning author of several women›s fiction, contemporary fiction, Christian fiction, Romance, erotica, and science fiction novels that plumb the depth of unique relationships and women›s issues. She is also a contributor to a New York Times bestseller, one of AALBC›s 100 Top Authors, a member of CVS Hall of Fame, Mercedes Benz Mentor Award Nominee, and the E. Lynn Harris Author of Distinction.

In addition to successfully cracking the code of landing a deal for herself and others with a major publishing house, she continues to "pay it forward" by organizing the annual Cavalcade of Authors which gives readers intimate access to the most accomplished writing talent today. She also serves as CEO of Macro Marketing & Promotions Group which offers aspiring and established authors assistance with ghostwriting, developmental editing, publishing, marketing, and other services to jump-start or enhance their writing careers. She also founded NK Tribe Called Success for her clients who participate in literary events and media advertising as a group and produce creative projects and anthologies.

www.naleighnakai.com

About the Knights of the Castle Series

Don't miss the hot new standalone series. The Kings of the Castle made them family, but the Knights will transform the world.

Book 1 - King of Durabia – Naleighna Kai

No good deed goes unpunished, or that's how Ellena Kiley feels after she rescues a child and the former Crown Prince of Durabia offers to marry her.

Kamran learns of a nefarious plot to undermine his position with the Sheikh and jeopardize his ascent to the throne. He's unsure how Ellena, the fiery American seductress, fits into the plan but she's a secret weapon he's unwilling to relinquish.

Ellena is considered a sister by the Kings of the Castle and her connection to Kamran challenges her ideals, her freedoms, and her heart. Plus, loving him makes her a potential target for his enemies. When Ellena is kidnapped, Kamran is forced to bring in the Kings.

In the race against time to rescue his woman and defeat his enemies, the kingdom of Durabia will never be the same.

Book 2 - Knight of Bronzeville – Naleighna Kai and Stephanie M. Freeman

Chaz Maharaj thought he could maintain the lie of a perfect marriage for his adoring fans … until he met Amanda. The connection between them should have ended with that unconditional "hall pass" which led to one night of unbridled passion. But once would never satisfy his hunger for a woman who could never be his. When Amanda walked out of his life, it was supposed to be forever. Neither of them could have anticipated fate's plan.

Chaz wants to explore his feelings for Amanda, but Susan has other ideas. Prepared to fight for his budding romance and navigate a plot that's been laid to crush them, an unexpected twist threatens his love and her life. When Amanda's past comes back to haunt them, Chaz enlists the Kings of the Castle to save his newfound love in a daring escape.

Book 3 - Knight of South Holland – Karen D. Bradley

Calvin Atwood has been the "go to" guy for members of the of Kings of the Castle. Partnering with Daron Kincaid on top-secret projects was great for achieving a career high, but now one new endeavor could put him in danger again. The first assignment as a Knight of the Castle was to create a military shield for the Kingdom of Durabia. No problem, since Calvin had been secretly working on something similar. Huge problem when countries who are at odds with the American government will stop at nothing to get their hands on him. Suddenly everything becomes complicated—including his parents' desire to suddenly pair him up with a former military man who doesn't seem above board.

Now every issue threatens to destroy his role as one of Knights of the Castle, and has Daron and his eight brother Kings questioning if Calvin is up to the task.

Book 4 - Lady of Jeffrey Manor – J. S. Cole and Naleighna Kai

When Blair Swanson, a surgical nurse from the American Midwest, arrives in the Kingdom of Durabia on assignment, she catches the eye of Crown Prince Hassan—one of the realm's most eligible bachelors.

His family has their own plans for an arranged marriage, and she discovers that love can transcend serious obstacles. But is the love between them strong enough to rise above the tyranny of others, the schemes of an ex-husband unwilling to let go, along with the ultimatum that forbids marriage between a commoner and a member of the royal family?

To complicate matters, a dark secret emerges that may change their lives forever.

Book 5 - Knight of Grand Crossing – Hiram Shogun Harris, Naleighna Kai, and Anita L. Roseboro

Rahm has a second chance at life after paying for a crime he didn't commit. With the support of his Aunt Alyssa, who never doubted his innocence, he emerges stronger than ever.

He's now living the life of his dreams as a Knight of the Castle with Marilyn, the perfect woman, by his side. Unfortunately, his blissful existence is threatened by family drama and someone from his past, who is set on revenge.

Through a chance encounter leading to a mysterious Bliss Event, Alyssa might find happiness with Ahmad Maharaj, a wealthy doctor with a complicated past and even more "complex" handle on intimate relationships. Susan, his new business partner, is on the rebound from a marriage that went sour, and has no plans to relinquish her newly-minted hold on Ahmad.

While Ahmad and Alyssa navigate personal issues, a frantic call from Rahm means finding a way to keep Marilyn and Alyssa safe with the help of the Kings of the Castle, as he deals with both domestic and international threats.

Book 6 - Knight of Paradise Island – J. L. Campbell

What happens when a second female expatriate turns up dead with several missing organs in an annex state of the Kingdom of Durabia?

Dorian "Ryan" Bostwick receives a one-of-a-kind assignment from his cousin, Shaz, the managing member and one of the Kings of the Castle which also reconnects him with Aziza Hampton, a summer love from his teen years. When she vanishes after an evening out with friends in Durabia's capital city, Ryan races against time to solve this ominous mystery and bring the perpetrators of the murders to justice before Aziza meets the same fate as all the others.

Book 7 - Knight of Irondale – J. L Woodson, Naleighna Kai, and Martha Kennerson

Neesha Carpenter is on the run from a stalker ex-boyfriend.

While fleeing the madness of that relationship, she discovers that Chicago Police sees her as the main suspect in his murder. With everything spinning out of control, she runs into Christian Vidal, a former classmate, who offers her a safe haven in the kingdom of Durabia. Neesha's relief doesn't last long, as her stay in the country causes an international incident and places the royal family at odds with the extradition laws of the American government. Christian is smitten with Neesha's strength, intelligence and beauty, and will do whatever it takes to keep her out of harm's way, including enlisting the help of the Kings of the Castle in America.

As more details surrounding the murder emerge, Christian will have to ask himself ... did she pull the trigger?

Book 8 - Knight of Birmingham – Lori Hays

As a dedicated advocate for single mothers with tragic pasts, Meghan Turner faces a sinister reality. She uncovers a disturbing pattern of missing mothers who were referred to "special treatment centers" before their release from the Alabama justice system. After reaching out to law enforcement for help, disaster hits close to home when her friend vanishes under those same mysterious circumstances.

While at a political fundraiser, Rory Tannous, overhears Meghan voicing her concerns with what seems to be orchestrated disappearances. The issues speak to his own past when his mother married, then disappeared the moment she and his siblings migrated to a volatile part of the world. He elicited the help of Daron Kincaid, King of Morgan Park, in his family's rescue and now needs to find Meghan's friend. Along the way, they discover a government alliance of powerful men willing to rid themselves of anyone who stands in their way.

The stakes are high, and discovery may lead to Rory and Meghan's destruction and the disappearance of vulnerable souls.

Book 9 - Knight of Penn Quarter – Terri Ann Johnson and Michele Sims

Following a successful FBI sting operation, Agent Mateo Lopez accepts a new assignment that takes him into the world of illegal adoptions between the United States and other nations.

Unfortunately, his love life suffers from the demands of his career. That is, until he meets the classy but "unlucky in love," Rachel Jordan, who has sworn off relationships and commits herself to running a children's social service agency and simpler pleasures. Mateo finds himself falling for her in more ways than one, and when trouble brews in one of Rachel's cases, he does everything in his power to keep her safe and protect the children from danger. Even if it means resorting to extreme measures.

Will the choices they make cost them their lives, or bring them closer together?

About the Kings of the Castle Series

"Did you miss The Kings of the Castle? "They are so expertly crafted and flow so well between each of the books, it's hard to tell each is crafted by a different author. Very well done!" - Lori H..., Amazon and Goodreads

Each King book 2-9 is a standalone, NO cliffhangers

Book 1 – Kings of the Castle, the introduction to the series and story of King of Wilmette (Vikkas Germaine)

USA TODAY, *New York Times*, and National Bestselling Authors work together to provide you with a world you'll never want to leave. The Castle.

Fate made them brothers, but protecting the Castle, each other, and the women they love, will make them Kings. Their combined efforts to find the current Castle members responsible for the attempt on their mentor's life, is the beginning of dangerous challenges that will alter the path of their lives forever.

These powerful men, unexpectedly brought together by their pasts and current circumstances, will become a force to be reckoned with.

King of Chatham - Book 2 – London St. Charles

While Mariano "Reno" DeLuca uses his skills and resources to create safe havens for battered women, a surge in criminal activity within the Chatham area threatens the women's anonymity and security. When Zuri, an exotic Tanzanian Princess, arrives seeking refuge from an arranged marriage and its deadly consequences, Reno is now forced to relocate the women in the shelter, fend off unforeseen enemies of The Castle, and endeavor not to lose his heart to the mysterious woman.

King of Evanston - Book 3 - J. L. Campbell

Raised as an immigrant, he knows the heartache of family separation firsthand. His personal goals and business ethics collide when a vulnerable woman stands to lose her baby in an underhanded and profitable scheme crafted by powerful, ruthless businessmen and politicians who have nefarious ties to The Castle. Shaz and the Kings of the Castle collaborate to uproot the dark forces intent on changing the balance of power within The Castle and destroying their mentor. National Bestselling Author, J.L. Campbell presents book 3 in the Kings of the Castle Series, featuring Shaz Bostwick.

King of Devon - Book 4 - Naleighna Kai

When a coma patient becomes pregnant, Jaidev Maharaj's medical facility comes under a government microscope and media scrutiny. In the midst of the investigation, he receives a mysterious call from someone in his past that demands that more of him than he's ever been willing to give and is made aware of a dark family secret that will destroy the people he loves most.

King of Morgan Park - Book 5 - Karen D. Bradley

Two things threaten to destroy several areas of Daron Kincaid's life—the tracking device he developed to locate victims of sex trafficking and an inherited membership in a mysterious outfit called The Castle. The new developments set the stage to dismantle the relationship with a woman who's been trained to make men weak or put them on the other side of the grave. The secrets Daron keeps from Cameron and his inner circle only complicates an already tumultuous situation caused by an FBI sting that brought down his former enemies. Can Daron take on his enemies, manage his secrets and loyalty to the Castle without permanently losing the woman he loves?

King of South Shore - Book 6 - MarZe Scott

Award-winning real estate developer, Kaleb Valentine, is known for turning failing communities into thriving havens in the Metro Detroit area. His plans to rebuild his hometown neighborhood are dereailed with one phone call that puts Kaleb deep in the middle of an intense criminal investigation led by a detective who has a personal vendetta. Now he will have to deal with the ghosts of his past before they kill him.

King of Lincoln Park - Book 7 – Martha Kennerson

Grant Khambrel is a sexy, successful architect with big plans to expand his Texas Company. Unfortunately, a dark secret from his past could destroy it all unless he's willing to betray the man responsible for that success, and the woman who becomes the key to his salvation.

King of Hyde Park - Book 8 -Lisa Dodson

Alejandro "Dro" Reyes has been a "fixer" for as long as he could remember, which makes owning a crisis management company focused on repairing professional reputations the perfect fit. The same could be said of Lola Samuels, who is only vaguely aware of his "true" talents and seems to be oblivious to the growing attraction between them. His company, Vantage Point, is in high demand and business in the Windy City is booming. Until a mysterious call following an attempt on his mentor's life forces him to drop everything and accept a fated position with The Castle. But there's a hidden agenda and unexpected enemy that Alejandro doesn't see coming who threatens his life, his woman, and his throne.

King of Lawndale - Book 9 - Janice M. Allen

Dwayne Harper's passion is giving disadvantaged boys the tools to transform themselves into successful men. Unfortunately, the minute he steps up to take his place among the men he considers brothers, two things stand in his way: a political office that does not want the competition Dwayne's new education system will bring, and a well-connected former member of The Castle who will use everything in his power—even those who Dwayne mentors—to shut him down.